VOLUME THREE

Airship 27 Productions

Pulp Mythology Volume Three

"The Tale of Sigurd's Name" © 2024 Teel James Glenn
"Hercules and the Wrath of the Red Sorceress" © 2024 Elizabeth Freeman
"John Henry Vs the Vampires" © 2024 Eric Esquivel
"The Lord's Work" © 2024 Harding McFadden and Iris Hawkins

Published by Airship 27 Productions
www.airship27.com
www.airship27hangar.com

Cover and interior illustrations © 2024 Ron Hill

Editor: Ron Fortier
Associate Editor: Gordon Dymowski
Marketing and Promotions Manager: Michael Vance
Production Designer: Rob Davis

ISBN: 978-1-953589-78-1

Printed in the United States of America

10 9 8 7 6 5 4 3 2 1

Volume Three

The Tale of Sigurd's Name
(A Viking Adventure)
BY TEEL JAMES GLENN

Gungir, Odin's spear, flashed across the sky with savage ferocity and turned the night bright as day. Unseen, Thor's hammer Mjolnr boomed in the angry distance. The Mediterranean Sea rose to mountainous heights driven by the wind and tossed the lone ship to and fro like giants juggling.

Sigurd the Luckless stood braced on the afterdeck of the imperial ship that was being buffeted by the storm and cursed. He was a giant even among his own northern race, with red-blond hair and a full red beard that dripped with the slanting rain. "I have earned my name again," he snarled to no one in particular.

It had been an ill trip from the beginning since the flotilla of six ships had left Constantinople for Alexandria. They had gone far out into the open sea to avoid contact with Syrian raiders but a sudden storm had blown up and scattered the ships so that he could not even see any of the other of the friendly vessels. In the darkness of the raging the storm and the mountainous sea around them there was no way to find any navigation points, stars or land. They were certainly lost, probably close to the African coast, but not exactly sure where.

"You seem upset, Sigurd," A feminine voice cut through the whistling wind and caused the northman to turn. "I thought you Varangian Guardsmen were all sailors, does a little storm like this frighten you?"

The girl who spoke was just barely in her teens with red hair darker than his. She was Sofia of Constantinople, niece of Emperor Nikephoros, with much the same features as her uncle but with darker skin, brighter eyes and a ready smile.

"I do not curse the storm, Lady Sofia." Sigurd said. "Just my luck to be—" He suddenly realized who he was talking to and hesitated.

The girl was beyond her years in her understanding of many things and flashed her warmest smile. "I know you would rather be fighting the Syrians than nursemaiding a spoiled child." In fact, the girl was anything but spoiled; strong willed, perhaps, but no more imperious in her manner than any others at court. In fact, often less so and more searching for the truth than many.

She had to speak loudly and lean in to be heard over the storm's growing fury. She did so in a way to show off her newly sprouted figure to maximum advantage.

Sigurd almost laughed at the teenager's attempt to flirt. She barely came to his broad chest. His ice blue eyes filled with humor at the girl's behavior.

"You are wise beyond your years, M'lady," Sigurd said, his deep voice cutting through the storm with no effort. "It is true I prefer to fight than chaperone, but you are not such an ogre nor a burden that I suffer-over much. You may be even more formidable than the Syrians."

The girl laughed. "A gallant deflection," she said. "You have learned much in my uncle's court." Suddenly her cheerful expression changed and she pointed to the horizon. "But you may get your wish to fight sooner than you thought."

The northman turned just as the lookout yelled, "Ships, ho!"

Sigurd cursed. "Syrian pirates!" Now he knew his luck was running true to form, first he was assigned to guard the girl by his commander Ragnar, then the ship separated from the rest of the escort fleet and now he had only six other fighting men on the luxury ship to fight not one, but two raider craft that were slicing through the violent waves.

"Lothar, Sven!" The red-haired giant called. "Full gear, prepare for borders!"

"Can we not outrun them?" Sofia asked with tension in her voice.

"If we had a dragon ship, perhaps," Sigurd said. "But these lumbering Byzantine ships handle like pregnant sows."

Despite the seriousness of their predicament the girl giggled. When she saw the sharp look the norseman gave her she added, "I wish I could fight beside you like Freya would."

At the mention of the Norse goddess of sex and war Sigurd smiled. "You are halfway there," he reassured her. "You have her courage. Now, please, lady, go below to safety, I beg you."

She accepted his compliment with a blush and without complaint. She nodded and crossed herself.

"Blessings of the Christ be upon you," she said, then whispered conspiratorially, "And of Odin." As she darted away the northman allowed himself a sly grin then turned his mind to the battle ahead.

The two Syrian craft were sleeker than the imperial ship and despite the storm were already moving to come upon their prey from two directions. They were sailors almost the equal of the northmen and they knew the waters of the Mediterranean.

"Here!" Lothar, a blond northman handed a spanghelm to Sigurd. "I know your head is hard, but you may still need this, brother."

Sigurd donned the helm and cursed again. "By Loki, my luck holds," he said. "This lumbering scow and its cargo left room for only we seven fighters."

"The crew will fight," Lothar offered, seriously as he tested the straps on his own helmet.

Both men looked at each other and then burst out laughing at the thought of the Byzantine seamen being any use in the coming battle. The two friends knocked their round shields together in salute.

"Oh, well," Sigurd offered with a hearty laugh, "Better than dying in bed."

He faced into the spray from the storm, gripped his axe and round shield and waited calmly beside his fellow Varangian guards along the railing of the ship.

Battles at sea, even in the chaos of a storm, were often tests of patience till the craft came within arrow shot of each other. It was good not to exhaust oneself in anticipation or fear.

So it was to be with this engagement. And the seven men from the cold climes of the north had no fear. They were experienced in war arts and had the patience of prey animals, able to wait with no twitch or tension until the moment came to strike with the speed of a great beast.

Sigurd and his men stood almost motionless on the deck while the crew of the ship worked frantically around them. The northmen might well have been statues of steel and stone, their weather-worn faces fixed on the approaching Arab ships with relaxed, even joyous expressions. Battle was in their blood and the real storm was within them when the time came for action.

The decks of the Syrian vessels were packed with fighting men. The northmen were easily outnumbered by ten or more to one and though such odds did not daunt them or dissuade them from looking forward to the battle, the outcome of such an encounter was in little doubt.

"Ragnar will be sorry he missed this fight," Sven, the lone Dane among the Swedes of the group said. "He was complaining last week of turning soft in Constantinople." Sven was shorter, darker and broader than the other six but had been in battle before with them so his courage and skill were not in doubt and he was accepted as one of them.

"He'll meet us in Valhalla soon enough," Sigurd said with a grim smile. "The way he cheats at dice someone will split his skull and send him to the Great Hall before long."

The seven warriors stood shoulder to shoulder in a tight wedge as the two raiders ships approached and rained down arrows on them.

"Shields!" Sigurd called as the shafts arced through the storm. The seven warriors raised their round wooden shields as one so that the arcing arrows thudded into them like so many wasps.

Several of the deck crew fell in the deadly shower but the seven protected by chainmail and helms remained unharmed. Then the Arab ships came close enough to toss grappling hooks and pull the three ships together. The rough seas made the task a hard one and the archers on the Byzantine ship were able to return several volleys of arrows to pepper the raiders before the ships came close enough for one of the Syrians to use boat hooks to pull on their prey. The hooks brought the gunwales against each other with a loud, violent collision.

"Hold!" Sigurd called as the Syrians swarmed onto the Byzantine ship.

Sigurd had time for one regret, that he would not be able to bring Sofia safely to the conclusion of their journey, then the Arabs and the northmen clashed with violence to dwarf the sound and fury of the thunder.

What followed was only hacking, cutting, blood and the horror of merciless battle.

The Varangian guard held their triangle formation for the first attack as if they were a sea wall repelling the pounding surf.

Axes swung, skulls cracked and salt spray became red with gore as lives ended with the collision with steel.

The Syrians wore lighter mail and had thin, curved swords and had chosen to fight without shields on the confines of shipboard for freedom of movement. The northmen's shields, helms, thicker chainmail and courage allowed them to withstand the onslaught without giving an inch. The northmen answered with axes and great, single handed hacking swords crying out with joyous abandon as they fought.

The northmen's armor turned the slender blade of the borders like ducks shedding water and their own straight broadswords cut down the Arabs like scythes through wheat with almost every swing. The first wave of Arabs fell in heaps at the defender's feet so that soon new invaders had to climb over the corpses of their brethren to hope for revenge.

The deck slicked with gore and salt water in equal parts.

The northmen were so efficient that soon they found no meat for their blades.

Maybe my luck is changing, Sigurd thought as he shook some brains from his axe.

Just then the second raider ship was driven into the Byzantium craft by a raging wave. The collision canted the deck violently so that even the northmen were thrown to their knees by the impact.

The attacking Arabs from the second ship cascaded over the gunwales and this time the defenders, their formation disrupted, were overwhelmed and forced into combat as individuals.

Still the northmen fought with the savage ferocity of wounded tigers knowing that capture meant slavery and no northman would live as a slave. These men would die in glory and sit in the Great Hall of All-Father Odin that night to feast and fight forever. There could be no greater or more prayed for fate.

The highborn on the Byzantine ship would be ransomed, their servants sold into bondage but if a Varangian guard could be captured alive he would fetch the highest price for any slave for the rarity of it.

It would never happen, of course; for the northmen it was victory or glorious death. And not one of them would have it any other way.

To his right Sigurd saw Lothar Iron Arm fall to a sword through the neck.

To his left Sven Olafson went down to a dozen deep cuts.

Then Gunnar Longaxe fell to a thrown knife.

And Erik Stoneface, Lars the Pale and Thor Steel Helm were hacked to pieces.

At last only Sigurd the Luckless fought on, ringed by a mound of dead and dying Syrians.

Sigurd's axe was abruptly wretched from his grasp, buried in the breastbone of one of his foes where it hooked and could not be wretched free. His shield splintered with a hard blow from a raider so he threw it into the face of an attacker.

At last Sigurd drew his sword and stood alone among his dead companions, facing the feral faces of the raiders. He challenged those leering faces with dark joy, "Come you sons of desert dogs! Let us make an end that they shall sing of till Ragnarok!"

The ring of Arabs actually drew back a moment as if sensing they fought not a man but an elemental force of nature; vengeance personified in a great red-haired beast!

Sigurd saw their hesitation and, fearing he might be robbed of his seat in Valhalla by a thrown ax or arrow, bellowed in his loudest voice, "Odin!" and charged.

The red giant was the reaper of death himself and ran over the first three foes before the others recovered from their shock at the mad counterattack of his whirling blade.

Arab arms were severed, faces crushed, swords broken but no blows of the Syrians reached the lone warrior who began to feel invincible.

"Are there no men in Syria?" he taunted.

At that instant the ships heaved again at the moment a curved blade embedded itself in Sigurd's spanghelm.

The northman saw stars and heard valkyries calling his name, "Sigurd the Luckless!" they said.

"Damn it!" the northman cursed. "Still luckless!"

Then there was a flash of light and darkness overwhelmed him!

†††

Sigurd became aware of floating and knew he was being born by shield maidens aloft to the Hall of the Gods. He wondered why he could not see the Great Hall then a gentle hand rubbed across his eyes and they opened to reveal a blue and cloudless sky. The sound of a roaring cheer reached his ears that he knew must be the cries of his fellow dead in the hall ahead of him.

Then the gentle hand returned and stung him in the open eyes and knew it was, "Sea water!"

He spat.

It was then, abruptly that his circumstance became clear to him. He was not being born aloft in the sky by the gatherers of the dead instead he was floating adrift in the sea, lying partially across a piece of flotsam, held in place by some tangle of rigging ropes across his chest.

He shook the lethargy from his consciousness and cursed. His helm was gone and the sting of the seawater on his scalp told him that he was wounded there. The stings in a dozen other places on his body told him he was hurt as well, but nothing that proclaimed any great damage.

"By Odin's beard," he screamed in anger and swallowed a mouthful of salt-water for his effort that got him coughing. "Luckless still!"

He also had the realization that while he was alive his fellows had perished and he had failed to protect Sofia. *And I will drown to boot!* he thought.

He moved his head and shrugged his massive shoulders, flexing his arms and legs to see the extent of his wounds but nothing screamed any great pain to him so with disgust he became certain there was no chance he would die of his battle earned wounds. *I will still not get to Valhalla!*

He turned his head to see that the sound he had first thought were cheers was the roar of waves on a rocky shore.

Thor's hand guided me here, he thought with hope, then with disgust added, *Or Loki's*. Like many of his fellow sailors Sigurd could not swim and, even if he could, his chainmail and hauberk would have pulled him to the bottom like an anchor.

The hand of the Norns that had woven his fate had arranged that he was trapped in the rigging from one of the damaged ships so effectively it was as if he had been purposely lashed to the wooden spar which was a section of one of the damaged masts. It had saved his life.

He became aware that the rocks ahead, where the pounding surf smashed itself to white foam, could still be the end of him. The spar with its human cargo was being tossed around in the surf and as it came closer to the shore the increased violence of the water dunked Sigurd several times. Each time he reemerged from the stinging seawater coughing and sputtering and he found himself closer to the jagged rocks.

Sigurd struggled to untangle his arms from the spar so he could control some of his fate. In what seemed like an eternity he felt the jarring impact as the spar was jammed into a crevasse between to rocks. He hung facedown like a roast on a spit with the water slapping him with each surge of the surf.

Fortunately he still had his dagger in its scabbard so he managed to use it to cut himself free from his ad hoc raft and cooking rack.

He dropped into knee-deep water when the ropes were sheared and crawled up onto the rocky sand of the beach coughing violently and spitting up water.

"Luckless!" He swore when he could breathe again. "Still Luckless."

It took the northman several minutes to be able to gather his strength stand and more still to get his 'land legs.'

He leaned against a seaweed-covered boulder and surveyed the stretch of beach he had landed on. It was a barren expanse barely a dozen feet deep, clearly only existed at low tide. He noted, with a sailor's eye that the tide was coming in, it was why he had been drawn into the rocky shore.

The narrow space was bordered by steep cliffs of composed of a blue-grey stone that looked to be mostly covered with moss.

There was no way for Sigurd to escape the landing spot except to climb out and he had to do it before the tide came in fully or he would be smashed against the mossy cliff face.

He knew his time was limited so he set about to escape. He used his dagger again to cut all the rope from the 'raft' and tied them together to create enough of a length of strong braided rope that should make it to the top of the cliff.

He created an X shaped 'hook' at the end of the rope with some small salvaged slivers from the spar he cut out with his knife.

"Looks like the only way I'll get to Valhalla is to climb there myself!" He said out loud. He stepped back and regarded the slick stonewall ahead of him.

It took him two-dozen tries to toss the improvised grapple to catch on an outcropping above him but when it did it held solid against a hard pull.

Sigurd discovered exactly where he had been injured in his shipboard ordeal in the next ten minutes as he climbed hand over hand up the rope. Every sore spot and bruise proclaimed itself as he ascended the cliff but only fueled his determination to make the top. The soles of his soft boots slipped and slid as he braced them against the mossy surface but he was used to a hard life and his aches could not trump his anger at still surviving.

After he reached the top of the cliff he lay exhausted on his stomach for at time to recover his strength. When he finally raised his head the sight that greeted the shipwrecked northman was an arid landscape stretching to a treeless, brown horizon.

Luckless still! He drew himself upright and looked back at the glassy sea then proclaimed aloud, "I live brothers, so I will raise a horn to you and take

...ARID LANDSCAPE STRETCHING TO A TREELESS BROWN HORIZON.

the heads of a hundred Syrians for each of you, I promise. Hold a place at the feast hall table for me, I will be there soon."

Then Sigurd began to walk inland keeping the sea to his behind and to the left as he moved forward at a steady, but easy pace.

The blazing sun began to suck the strength from the bearded giant from the very first step but he resisted the urge to remove his mail, despite its weight with his natural northern reluctance to risk dying 'out of harness.'

As the shadows grew the steps of the giant slowed yet he pushed on.

Sigurd knew he had to find water soon in order to live and his best bet to find it was to continue along the coast where he might find the outlet of a river or stream were it entered into the ocean. Even a salt march would point the way inland to a fresh water source. It was a question if he could find that outlet before he was little more than a dried out piece of leather.

The suddenness of nightfall forced the warrior to halt, lest in the inky black of the north African night he walk off a cliff or break an ankle in a crevasse.

The sandy soil along the coast held none of the heat of the day so the temperature dropped rapidly from sizzling heat to bone chilling cold with remarkable speed. He was glad he had elected to keep his chain and hauberk on then for they helped to insulate him.

He found a cleft in a rock where he wedged himself in tightly, all but collapsing from exhaustion. The small space helped him stay warm and he was so tired that the uncomfortable position made little difference. He dozed for a time till the quarter moon rose above the horizon. He felt rested enough that he was able to force himself to walk on by the pale blue light.

The briskness of the cold revived the northman and he pushed on with a more steady pace though still found had had to be careful because of the broken nature of the landscape. The moon-cast shadows added danger to the strangeness of the counryside.

The pace and need to stay alert kept him warm without sapping his vitality like the sun had. It was almost pleasant after his long hot day and reminded him of moonlit walks in his far away homeland.

If I must endure more of this Africa, he thought, *I shall move out at night and rest by day in some shadowed hole like a mole.* It was a good plan but he did not fool himself with false hope, he knew that without water even his Herculean physique would last no more than a day or two. The grumbling of his stomach in hunger was something he had felt before so that he did ignore, for now.

He kept a steady pace the whole night, keeping a weather eye for even scrub growth. His family ran a farm stead back in his native Sweden and so he knew that any plant would indicate water hidden beneath the sandy soil. Even with his dagger he was confident he could carve his way to that water should he plants.

As he walked the stranded sailor's mind went to his fallen comrades. He remembered their mirth, the fury of their battle rages and yet the gentleness and honesty that was at the core of their wyrd as well.

His fallen companion Lothar had taken a Byzantine wife in the last year, a little dark haired thing who had gentled her husband, to much ribbing from his fellows. Only two moons ago they had all learned she was with child and Lothar's joy had been a beautiful thing to behold.

"She will not want while I live," Sigurd promised to the starry sky, "and that child will know what a warrior their father was, this I vow."

As if in answer to his statement, a storm, far out across the sea boomed mutedly with a flash of lightning.

The northman smiled, seeing in his mind's eye Lothar drinking deep in the Hall of the Dead and took comfort in his own survival. He could, if he made it back to Constantinople, at least do a service for his friend. That made Sigurd feel alittle less luckless.

Before Sigurd realized it dawn had pinked the sky and the air began to heat up. He looked around for a shadowed spot to rest for the day and saw a depression in the land ahead of him. He also heard a sound that made his heart beat faster: gurgling water!

He quickened his steps till he stood at a wide cleft in the rocky highland he stood on, below which he could see a finger of the sea that cut into the land. It was clear to his nautical eye that it was not just an inlet of the sea but actually the delta of some river!

The northman searched the incline of the plateau for a way down with excitement that gave new strength to his legs. Eventually he found a gentle enough slope to descend carefully to sea level.

His first taste of the water proved it still salty from tidal backwash so he allowed himself to take only a small sip, sloshing the water around his mouth enough to absorb some then spit the rest out.

He followed the sluggish water inland till he stumbled around a bend in the tributary and came upon an unexpected scene: a tableau that was a still life on the edge of horror.

Ahead in the depression, which was more a small canyon, was a pool of water. The body of water was formed by a cascade of clear bubbling water from the plateau above. It was at the apex of that small canyon creating a small oasis with bushes and a small tree beside the pool of fresh water.

The northman's attention however was not on the life-saving liquid but on two figures who stood frozen on either side of the small pool; one was a young boy in long black and blue robes with several gourds scattered around him and the other was a black maned lion.

The king of beasts was crouched low, its gums pulled back to expose his yellowed teeth and its eyes focused on the human prey.

Neither figure moved and the only sound was the gurgling of the waterfall.

Sigurd's first instinct was to reach for his sword but, of course it was gone. He reached for his dagger then and drew it. It was barely larger than some of the teeth of the snarling lion.

It seems I will drink with you tonight afterall, Lothar, he thought as he slowly moved forward. *Someone else will have to look to your lady.*

Both the lion and the boy perceived the northman at the same moment.

The boy uttered a single gasp, the great cat a long, low growl.

"Come, beast," Sigurd challenged in a booming voice. "Leave that morsel and try for a stomach bursting feast!"

The lion roared an answer, shifting his full focus to the new intruder. He began to slink forward toward Sigurd its head lowered, its teeth fully bared.

The red-haired giant felt his pulse quicken and his muscles tense.

Here was a challenge.

A tingle of fear coursed through Sigurd, not a fear at the prospect of death for he embraced Hel, goddess of the afterlife. It was for the fear that the great beast might only cripple him then turn on the boy. He felt he had already failed the girl, he wold not fail the boy, that much he must assure did not happen.

"When he attacks me," Sigurd called in Greek, "Run for the cliff, I have heard these animals do not climb."

The boy's face was an impassive mask so the northman had no way of knowing if the boy understood Greek but had no time to ponder further as the great beast charged the northman.

✝✝✝

Time seemed to slow as the massive carnivore raced at Sigurd.

To the northman it seemed bigger than Fenris, the world devourer wolf, its jaws like a cavern, its fangs like stalagmites and its fiery eyes like burning suns.

Sigurd braced himself, crouching low; his whole being focused on the monster that was sprinting toward him. He assessed it as he would any foe, searching for weaknesses.

The first thing he noticed was that it was an old lion, its mane looking ragged and missing some of its teeth. There was desperation behind the fury in its eyes. And yet it was clear that it hunted human prey because it was at the end of its long life. It no longer was able to hunt fast or strong prey so it was almost reduced to scavenging. Humans were just a cut above the leavings of other predators.

Sigurd took in all this with a single look, *So we both want a noble end, eh, friend?* He thought just as the cat sprang.

The beast pounced with the intention to land on the human annoyance with its fore paws and tear at him with its powerful claws.

Sigurd, true to his natured, did not wait to accept the attack with passivity. Instead the northman threw himself forward at the same time the great cat leapt.

The lion was suddenly confused by a prey that did not flee, but instead twisted in the air to avoid the direct attack.

The northman ducked beneath the forepaws and stepped in to meet the beast before the apex of its leap, using his left arm to shield his head. Sigurd rammed his shoulder into the belly of the beast and drove his dagger in deep with all his might. He used all his strength and the monster's momentum to disembowel the creature with a long slice of the dagger.

The flailing hind claws of the lion raked at northman's hauberk and thighs opening deep wounds on the man's legs. The pain for both combatants was blinding but as was their feral nature neither conceded.

The lion landed in a pool of its own entrails and gore, spinning to strike at its tormentor-prey with now-feeble forepaws and a last, angry roar.

Sigurd screamed a cry that was half battle cry and half agony and slashed at the taloned paws of the dying monster.

The lion recoiled in new pain and the red-haired giant now launched himself at the beast, the hunted turned hunter, and landed on the lion's back. Sigurd locked his legs around the lion's body and began to stab repeatedly into its side.

The cat rolled trying to dislodge the man clinging to its back by squirming and twisting but the northman was unrelenting.

The knife blade flashed up and down in a spray of red chaos. Sand and gore were a mist around the roiling fighters and the roar of the now dying lion was like living thunder.

Then suddenly the beast did nothing but twitch and was silent.

Sigurd rolled from the lion's back, an avatar of destruction coated with the life of the great beast. He lay staring at the blue sky, every breath like fire in his lungs.

A youthful face appeared to block the sky.

"Sofia?" Sigurd muttered and then the world went black again.

†††

Sigurd opened his eyes hoping to see mead horns and hear the clash of blades but instead he saw a blue veiled man staring down at him who said in Greek, "You live!"

"Odin's spear!" Sigurd cursed. "Luckless again!"

The northman attempted to sit up but the strange blue face was attached to an arm and held him down. "Rest, warrior," the face said, "Your wounds are grievous and must heal."

Sigurd tried to protest but found he had no strength to do so. He was suddenly taken by a great weariness and closed his eyes again.

The wounded northman woke and slept numerous times over the next days so that he experienced the two as a tumble of images and sensations. There were other blue veiled men and delicate dark eyed women. There was also the same young face of the boy that Sigurd had rescued and mistaken for Sofia in the aftermath of the battle.

Then he in a haze he saw Sofia, but the girl was back in her uncle's court, in full court finery, yet she had a fighting axe in her hand and she held a round shield. "I am ready to fight beside you," the girl said. "But just tell me who to fight!"

There was also a grey bearded, one-eyed figure who the northman knew was the All-Father.

"Why are you not drinking in the hall with me tonight?" Odin said.

"I do not know," a frustrated Sigurd said, "I have tried many times to die with honor, my Father."

"What fun would that be?" A second, high-pitched, petulant voice said. "He's much more amusing on Midguard."

"Quiet, Loki!" A third, booming voice said. "There is still much for him to do before he joins us to feast."

Sigurd knew instinctively who that voice was and cried out, "Lord Thor, I can't do much while I'm on my back!"

"Then get up, man!" The red bearded god of thunder said, "And stop wasting time!"

Sigurd sat up.

"Ow!" The red-haired northman said.

Sigurd looked around. He was in a tent on a sleeping pallet and he was alone. He was also naked though there were bandages on half a dozen places on his body, most prominently on his thighs and around his chest.

Sigurd staggered to his feet and tottered unsteadily to the center pole of the tent. His wounds burned but the mighty thewed warrior ignored them as he tried to make sense of where he was.

"Ahyah!" a shrill yell drew his attention to the tent flap as a dark-haired girl screamed and ran from the tent. There followed moments of chaos and noise outside and other yells.

Sigurd looked around for a weapon, seizing on an oil lamp that was shaped like a ship.

"No need for that, warrior," a now familiar voice said in Greek. "You are among friends." The blue masked face that Sigurd had seen before his delirium entered the tent and smiled. He was masked and robed in blue, with startling blue eyes and a skin tinged as well with the dye of his clothing. He held his hands out palm up to show he was no threat.

The northman still held onto the pole for support but lowered the lamp.

Just then the boy Sigurd had saved pushed past the man. He seemed even younger than he had in the canyon, with a bright grin and slight figure.

"You are well, boy?" Sigurd asked in Greek. The boy looked at the naked giant wide eyed and nodded.

"My son, Humaydi is well, thanks to you, warrior," the masked man said as he lowered his face covering to show a thick black beard and a wide smile mirroring the boy's. "I am Moctar Ag Barha, chief of this tribe of Imuhagh, though the Athenians call us Tuareg. How are you called?"

"I am Sigurd called the Luckless," the northman said. He released the lamp and slid to the floor still holding on the pole. "And I am afraid I am tired."

"I am not surprised, Sigurd," Moctar said. He motioned to his son who moved into the tent and filled a cup with sweet wine and offered it to a grateful Sigurd.

"How is it you speak the Greek tongue?" The northman asked. He held up his empty cup and the boy obligingly refilled it, his eyes and smile still wide as he regarded the sailor's capacity as much as his size.

"We have traded with many of their ships in the port of Bechar." The Tuareg leader accepted a cup of wine from his son and sipped it. "Since I negotiate for my people it is good to learn the language. One day my son will do so, thus he is learning it as well." Sigurd could see that the man smiled easily. "And it is good you thought to call your warning in it." He held up the cup in toast. "No man can give enough thanks for the life of his son, but I will try with all I have."

The northman felt himself getting drossy from the effects of the wine and his wounds, a fact that Moctar noted. "You must rest now; we will have clothes brought to you so as not to frighten any more of our girls when you awaken next, I fear you will cause them to expect too much from their future husbands." He laughed at his on joke and it was a pleasant sound for the wounded warrior to fall asleep to.

Sigurd slept this time a deep and healing sleep that lasted a full day round. When he woke next, true to his word, Moctar had loose trousers and a robe waiting for the northman.

The red-haired giant was ravenously hungry as well when he woke and said so. The Tuareg leader sent several men to assist Sigurd to come to his tent for a dinner in his honor but he would have none of their assistance. He made his way to Moctar's main pavilion on his own unsteady feet where the feast was to be held.

Humaydi sat beside Sigurd and his father and translated for his savior. The other men spoke to the northman, praising his courage and made many jokes about the young boy finding 'strange pets.' The men, who had remained veiled outside the tent lowered their veils inside, a mark, Sigurd found, of their respect for him. The men of the Imuhagh always wore their veils in the presence of outsiders to their community.

The desert dwellers were amazed by Sigurd's return to vitality from wounds that they were sure would have killed most men. The northman took their praise with laconic acceptance adding, "it seems I can not find my way to Valhalla no matter how hard I try."

This puzzled his host but no one dwelled on it as the food was served. The feast consisted of dates, sweet breads, lamb and other exotic delicacies.

The desert folk had as many questions for the red-haired giant as he had for them. When they asked him to explain why he was called 'Luckless' he replied, "I was a farmer who became a sailor to go a Viking, then a bodyguard. Now I am a land locked in a place that can grow no crops and the Emperor's niece whom I was to guard lies dead at the bottom of the ocean; could I have any worse luck?"

Humaydi translated to the other men and they all found it amusing save for one who spoke to the boy.

"You are wrong," the young Tuareg said. "Abdullah Ag Matta says this girl is not dead."

The northman sat up at that. "Do not jest with me about that; it is a bitter thing for one who has sworn on an oath ring to fail in that oath."

"But he does not jest, oh Lion Killer," Humaydi insisted. "Abdullah says he saw her this very week past in Bechar. There were Syrian ships that have come to port; they were damaged by the storm. And as the caliph fears the Syrians he has welcomed them as guests in his fortress while their ships are to be repaired and made sea worthy again."

"What has this to do with Sofia?" Sigurd demanded, leaning forward so swiftly it startled the boy.

"They had with them a person of great value, Abdullah says," the boy continued. "The word in the bizarre was that the person was a girl of high rank with hair the color of fire much as yours."

"By *Mjolnr*!" the northman swore on the thunder god's hammer. "It is Sofia! This means I must go to Bechar and free her or die in the attempt!"

"ABDULLAH AG MATTA SAYS THE GIRL IS NOT DEAD."

The red-haired giant's outburst startled the feast goers but when Humaydi explained his reasons to them the mood grew even more festive; revenge and duty were two things the desert folk understood very well. Their respect for the giant grew with the intensity of his dedication.

"Despite your protests to the contrary, Sigurd," Moctar said with the calm manner of a leader who saw the bigger picture. "You are still healing and can do little as you are. It is normally a two-day journey to Bechar if one rides steadily. Thusly I think it would be better if we went slowly that you may gain full strength."

"Yet I will go," Sigurd said with steely determination. "I must go."

"And so you will," the desert leader said. "But you must rest one more day while we prepare to take our wares to market in our regular monthly; we will do so a little early which will serve you well getting you into the city. The trip will take four days. You will come with us, disguised as one of our tribe to enter the town unseen."

The red bearded giant was moved by the chief's words and took a moment to reply. When he did speak he was almost choked with emotion. "I do not ask you to risk your people to pay my blood debt," Sigurd said. "You must continue to trade with these people, I would not jeopardize that by involvement with me. I do not know what will happen when I arrive at Bechar but I can not but think it will be bad."

"And you will not jeopardize our trade, my friend," Moctar said. "As a chief my people must not be involved, but as a father I have my own blood debt to pay. All is in the hands of Fate. We will talk no more of it now; eat, enjoy and rest. Then we prepare."

Sigurd followed the chief's advice, drank and jested and ate heartily at the feast with men who, though they outwardly looked so different he felt a sudden and deep kinship with. Yet shadows lurked behind the red-haired giant's eyes.

The words of Thor form his vision, "There is still much for him to do before he joins us to feast." Echoed in Sigurd's mind.

Yes, he thought, *there is much to do but by my heart I will do it.*

Sigurd slept much of the next day but when he was awake he was possessed by nervous energy that could not be contained. He was given one of the Tuareg swords and spent his waking time getting the feel of the lighter weapon and testing the limits of his recovery. His ribs were sore, probably cracked and his legs shaky, but he would not be daunted in his attempt to be ready for his one-man assault on the city.

Humaydi stayed by the northman's side the whole day, apparently fascinated by everything the red-haired giant did.

"Have you really sailed the ocean sea?" the boy asked while Sigurd was resting in the shade outside his tent.

"Many times," the northman said. "Even to the Greenlands to the far west." The northman had set up a roll of old carpets and straw to use as a practice pell. Within very few moments of his work on the target it was slashed to pieces.

"Is the ocean sea very big?"

"As big," Sigurd smiled as he sipped from a gourd of water, "As your sea of sand."

"So very big?" The boy exclaimed.

"Maybe bigger!"

"I think nothing is bigger," Humyadi said. "You will see when you travel across it to Bechar."

"You do not travel with us?" Sigurd asked.

"Father says the danger is too great this time," the boy said. "The Syrians are not liked by the people and the caliph; he thinks you may anger them."

"I shall try to."

The boy was silent for a time as if thinking deep thoughts then said, "I have made something for you." He held up a necklace with a dozen gleaming white objects stitched together on a line of black silk cord.

"They are the teeth of the lion you slew." He puffed up his chest with pride then added shyly, "It is to remember me."

The northman took the gift and placed it around his neck with reverence. He reached to his side and removed his dagger and scabbard. "Then you must take this which slew the beast to remember me."

"I will never forget you," Humaydi said with deep feeling. He caressed the dagger as if it was the greatest treasure that had ever been. And to him it was.

"Nor will I forget you," the northman said. "These are gifts between men; warrior brothers who have faced Hel and survived."

"Warrior brothers?" the boy said, eyes wide with awe. His face got red with emotion and he suddenly stood and raced off holding the dagger to his chest as one would a suckling child.

"Warrior brothers, indeed." Sigurd watched him go and was tempted to laugh till he touched the teeth on the necklace and his face lit in a warm smile instead. "May I have your courage in facing the Syrians you had facing me."

†††

The port town of Bechar was hardly a metropolis. It was a collection of mud brick buildings around the mouth of a small river in a natural estuary. Overlooking it was a faint attempt at a fortress-palace on a sheer cliff that jutted out over the water like barnacle on a ship.

Moctar Ag Barha led his small caravan on a slow march across the desert to the town, during which Sigurd slept in the saddle most of the way. By the time they were at the low gate of the town the red-haired giant was feeling mostly himself and ready to meet his fate.

The estuary had two piers that were thrust out into the bay with small fishing boats docked and several more rounding the point preparing to land.

"There are the Syrian ships," Abdullah pointed to a salt marsh where two ships were partly dry-docked off to the side of the small port area.

"We have come none-to-soon," the northman said as he assessed the craft with an experienced eye. "They look to be seaworthy or close to it."

Sigurd rode with the Tuaregs dressed as one of them in long robes with a face veil. He was indistinguishable from them save for his unusual height which he took pains to disguise by slumping. Even his blue eyes would not give him away as many of the Imuhagh also had them.

The two-dozen desert dwellers and their packhorses attracted no special attention as they passed two drossy guards at the outer edge of the town.

"They have no defenses," Sigurd noted quietly when they group had passed into the town.

"From the desert they do not need them," Moctar said. "The caliph's fort on that spit of land can be held by very few from many. The town is on its own." He laughed. "There is little enough to steal in it to interest even poor raiders. It is just a place to replenish water from the springs that burst from the underground rivers that empty to the catch basin, refit boats and then move on."

The bazaars of the town lined the narrow streets beneath cloth covers and were meagerly stocked. Still what was there showed the diversity of wares as there was something, it seemed, from every culture on the Mediterranean and from beyond somewhere on the shelves.

Moctar pointed to the road from the town that led to the spires of the fortress. "There are guards on the path upward to the fortress," he said. "They are Syrians placed there by their ship commanders. They trust no one."

"They know the town does not like them," Abdullah added with a derisive laugh. "They never move among the people down below but in groups for fear of getting their throats slit by an uprising."

While Moctar Ag Barha negotiated with locals for the dates and other desert wares and for imported goods in return Sigurd hung back among the band and observed every detail of the town. The band of Tuaregs moved easily as a unit and the northman, slumping to blend in, moved with them, memorizing the streets and surrounding area for possible use later.

He also became aware that there was an atmosphere of tension in the town, a ripple of nervousness beneath the day-to-day activities. Sigurd saw it come to the surface when any of the Syrians, always in groups of three or four, swaggered down the street going to the dock or the fortress.

The Arab interlopers acted more like conquerors than stranded guests as they moved through the marketplace. The townsfolk cast furtive glances at the armored Syrians, muttering curses behind their backs as they walked by indicating what they wanted to be brought down to their ship. 'The Caliph will pay for this." the Arabs said time and again but never paid in coin themselves.

To Sigurd it was clear they were provisioning for sea, he had indeed come to Bechar just in time if he was to do anything to find and save the girl.

The nortman turned his attention to the fortress itself.

It was placed at the very tip of a precipice overlooking the port, atop a sheer cliff. There was only a single, narrow road which had two alert looking guards standing at a gate at its foot and more standing at attention by the gate of the fort itself.

"No approach from the road," Sigurd thought, "except by stealth at night, but then they will be expecting such an approach." He looked at the area around the fortress for some other access and then smiled beneath his veil as he began to form a plan.

"I would like you to purchase a few things for me, Moctar," he said. "I will find a way to pay you back."

"Please, do not insult me, warrior," the chief said. "What it is you require?"

"Rope, a dozen iron spikes such as are used in ship building and a wooden mallet."

"It will be done, Sigurd." Moctar said, "But as you can see it is impossible to enter the fortress by the road, it is well guarded and at night they will close the gate."

"But the cliff is not guarded."

"I know you feel obligated to try to reach this woman, but to reach the fortress you would have to be a bird and fly, my friend."

"Or be carried by valkyrie," the northman said with a chuckle.

When the Tuareg band left the town before sunset there was one less in their number. Sigurd attempted to thank Moctar for his help, but the desert chief had silenced him with "You have given me my posterity. All debts are paid. May your gods as well as ours watch over you."

Sigurd watched them ride away feeling almost as if he were losing his ship-mates again, but he put the emotion aside and set about on his mission.

He'd hidden at the edge of the town till nightfall then moved stealthily to the base of the cliff on which the fortress sat. He shed his robes under which he still wore his mail and lion-scared hauberk. He kicked off his soft desert boots and sheathed his sword on his back, coiling a length of rope over it then began to climb. The night was moonless so the warrior had no fear of being seen from the town or from the fortress because of the overhang of the cliff.

Sigurd stretched to limber up then began to move up the rock wall with the sureness of a lizard.

In the daylight he had seen that the seemingly 'unscalable' rock cliff was, in fact as climbable as the fjords he had climbed back home in his youth, some twenty years ago. He would often climb ahead of the other boys to watch for ships returning from Viking and though he was bigger and heavier than those days his grip strength and endurance was greater as well.

The tiny cracks and crevasses were as easy for him to use to climb as if they had been a ladder. He was able to fit his fingers and toes into most of the cracks, but when he could not he used the iron spikes and the mallet, which he had wrapped in leather to muffle the sound of strikes to create finger holds.

It was slow going and Sigurd's wounds began to ache fiercely, but it only spurred him on. He knew he had to make the fortress by dawn or he would be spotted with certainty from the town. As he progressed, he also knew he could not go back down he would never be able to retrace his way down in the darkness. It was an all or nothing gamble. It was a race to the top, but he had to be methodical and careful, for one misstep would mean a fatal fall. It was a challenge he relished.

His plan once he reached the top was only roughly formed and simple; reach the fort, find the girl and somehow, against all the odds, escape.

They will not expect someone to come for Sofia, He consoled himself. *That is something.*

As the night wore on his muscles began to tire and cramp. He began to worry that he might not actually make it to the top before the sun revealed him to his enemies.

I was a boy a long time ago, he thought wryly as it seemed every muscle in his massive frame was screaming in pain. Nonetheless he kept on climbing, inexorably, excruciatingly toward the top.

Gradually Sigurd became aware that he could see the rockface before him with greater, if sporadic detail. *It can not be the dawn already*, he thought with a sense of panic welling within him.

He chanced to look over his shoulder and he discovered the source of the light, lightning!

Out on the horizon the flashes of lightning could be seen and as if a frost giant was whispering the following boom of thunder made its way to him. It was a big storm and it was moving rapidly across the water toward the shore. And toward the climbing man who was completely exposed.

Sigurd climbed with increased urgency but had to be careful not to rush. His fingertips were bloody by this time and every muscle in his body was crying out for rest but he knew he could not, so he pressed on.

The wind off the sea echoed the cold drafts of those fjords of his youth.

The stinging rain began. It pelted him with icy droplets that were like the sting of so many bees but he pressed on. There was no thought but to climb. No feeling but to continue upward.

Flashes of lightning seemed so close that Sigurd could smell the burnt air after the blast of the bolt.

Then the rumble of thunder boomed so loud that it almost shook him from the side of the cliff.

"Damn you, Loki," Sigurd yelled. "This storm is your doing!"

In answer to his curse the fury of the storm seemed to double in intensity.

Sigurd continued to climb, now propelled by anger.

"I will not die luckless!" He snarled. "Do you hear me, Trickster? I will not!"

At last he was at the foot of the fortress wall. He paused to drive several spikes into the edge of the cliff to use as a base for him to grip. Then he uncoiled the rope on his back which he had already tied into a loop.

Leaning back he swung the rope and, against the force of the driving wind and rain both, threw the loop upward at the crenellated top of the wall.

The wind and rain worked against him, but also made it less likely a guard would be making normal rounds and thus discover him. On the fifth toss the loop held.

Sigurd gathered himself and climbed the rope, walking up the mud-brick wall in relative ease compared to his arduous climb up the cliff.

When the northman hurled himself over the parapet to crash to the walkway beyond he had no strength left and just lay exhausted on his back, breathing hard. He could not even rise to his feet when an enterprising captain of the guard rounded the corner of the wall and spotted him!

†††

The watch captain was so startled to see the drenched and bedraggled giant lying in his path that for a moment he could not even react. When he did think to yell for the guards a boom of thunder drowned out the sound of his scream of alarm.

In that instant Sigurd hurled his wooden mallet with all the force he could muster. The hammer struck the soldier directly in the head, felling him like a dropped stone.

The northman was on the stunned man immediately and muttered "Tis not *Mjolnr* but will do!"

Sigurd pulled the still dazed captain to the edge of the wall overlooking the sea and hoisted him bodily over his head with relative ease.

"Where is the female prisoner the Syrians brought?" He asked in Greek.

He had to shake the man and repeat his question twice before the suspended man squeaked, "In the seraglio, there—" He pointed to a part of the fortress that rose to a tower.

"Good," Sigurd said.

"You will let me go now?" The captain asked.

"No," Sigurd said. Then with no more thought to the man he tossed the soldier over the wall to fall into the sea, his screams of horror were lost in the fury of the storm.

The northman, his goals set, drew his sword, his aches forgotten. He moved along the parapet, crouching low, until he stood beneath the raised part to the fort that the captain indicated. There were no guards in sight as he slunk along the wall looking for a way up to the woman's quarters.

My luck must be turning, He allowed himself to think.

He paused at a setback in the wall to reconsider what to do next when a sudden flash of celestial brightness exposed Sigurd in stark relief against the base of the wall. At that moment a group of guards rounded the far corner of the seraglio wing.

The guards reacted instantly when they saw the intruder by drawing their swords and charged.

Sigurd's first thought was to face the group, steel to steel, but the lightning flash also revealed that there was a narrow door at the back of the shadowed setback behind him. The northman made a split second decision and dashed for the dark spot, gambling that the door was enterable.

It was!

Sigurd squeezed his bulk through the carelessly unlocked door to find himself on a landing of a staircase. He slammed the door behind him and threw the bolt just as the guards collided with the outside of the portal. The soldiers pounded on the door and began screaming for their fellows.

HE TOSSED THE SOLDIER OVER THE WALL.

So much for stealth, the red-haired giant thought as he raced up the stairs. *I must find Sofia swiftly or all is lost.*

The landing he stood on gave him a choice, up or down a narrow set of stairs. He chose to ascend which brought him to another door. That door disgorged him onto a wide, carpeted corridor lined with luxurious tapestries hung along its walls.

Sigurd moved cautiously, for anyone of the hangings could hide danger behind it. The seraglio seemed an endless maze of intersecting hallways and barred doors. He could faintly hear the sound of the storm outside the thick walls of the building and heard, or imagined he heard, the sound of the alarm being raised.

The northman began to dispair of locating Sofia before the Syrians came to secure their prize when it occurred to him that was exactly what he did want.

As he had the thought he heard the tread of marching feet approaching around a bend in the corridor. He darted behind a tapestry and waited.

A detachment of Syrians flew down the corridor past him, not looking for him but intent on reaching some destination. It was just what he had hoped for. Four of the men broke off from the marching group at the barked order from a unit commander before the rest of the group moved on at a swfit jog.

The four detached men took up position on either side of one of the barred doors Sigurd had tried earlier to no success.

"they guard their prize," Sigurd thought with a wolfish grin. "But they have no idea from whom they guard it or they would have all stayed."

The northman slipped along the wall, shielded by the tapestry but careful not to move swiftly enough to make the hanging reveal his presence. Moving slowly this way he was able to get within a dozen feet of the four guards, but no closer.

The northman did not hesitate then, he pulled the last iron spike from his belt and threw it high and hard over the heads of the guards. It flew above the level of light cast by the wall sconces to land far down the hall with a loud thud.

The four guards all turned as one to react to the sound.

Sigurd charged the guards' back and struck down two before they even knew he was there.

The two remaining Arabs were no match for the fury of the red-haired giant and in five strokes they lay dead at his feet. None of the guards had time to call out alarm but Sigurd could not be sure the commotion had not been heard.

The northman quickly broke the lock on the door they had been guarding and entered the room.

Only a lifetime of violence saved him from what happened next.

A vase flew straight at the northman's head which he dodged by inches. The pottery was followed by a cry of, "Sigurd!"

The northman almost swung his sword as a red-haired dynamo launched herself into his arms and hugged him fiercely. "I thought you were dead!" Sofia yelled.

Sigurd allowed himself to enjoy the girl's joy, that almost mirrored his own, then said, "I almost was, little Freya, from your mighty toss!"

The girl blushed and jumped down from his embrace but held onto his arm. "I'm sorry," she said.

"Don't be," he smiled genuinely pleased, "Shield maidens never apologize!"

He noticed for the first time that the girl was dressed in colorful silks that almost revealed more than they concealed of her budding figure. On her feet were gold slippers.

"We have to move swiftly," the giant said. "They know someone is in the fort."

The girl nodded as they moved to the door. "On the ship I saw the lightning hit the ship and you— it was like the hand of God— lifted you from the deck and threw you into the sea!"

"A god, indeed," Sigurd said. He knew that if he had fallen on the ship the Syrians would have brained him and he would not have made it to Sofia's side. He heard the echo of Thor's words "There is still much for him to do."

"What do we do now?" Sofia asked, interrupting his musings.

The northman hesitated to answer, partly because he was not sure himself. His plan, what there had been of it, had only to find the girl and escape. The fine points of how to escape were not very well worked out. He decided she didn't need to know that.

"We get out of this fortress," he said matter-of-factly, "Even with them sure there is someone has broken in they will not expect us to leave so soon." He did his best to sound hopeful.

"You don't really believe that, do you?" the girl asked.

He shrugged. "You are too smart for a young girl, Sofia. Are you sure you're not a Rhine dwarf in disguise?"

She playfully punched his arm. "I am a young woman!" she pointed out. "And you came for me, that is all that matters."

"Well at least we have to get out of here."

They went out into the corridor through the door he had entered. When Sofia saw the four dead guards and gave a little gasp. Instead of saying anything, however, she bent and retrieved a long Kindjal dagger from one of the men's belts. In her hand the long knife looked like a full-sized sword.

"Little Freya," Sigurd whispered with approval.

The odd pair moved down the hallway with the girl directing.

"There are stairs going down to the other women's quarters," she said.

The northman led the way with his sword pointing ahead. Sofia held his left hand in her right, gripping her knife at the ready in her own left.

At the end of the long hallway the door to the stairway was ajar. The fugitives paused while Sigurd listened intently. From below came the sound of sharp commands in a harsh male voice then the sound of booted feet ascending.

Sigurd was about to head back the way they had come but cries from behind them meant the dead guards had been discovered.

"Up!" He hissed and the two fugitives race up the spiral staircase, his bare and her slippered feet making barely any sound.

The sound of the soldiers stopped at the floor the fugitives had escaped from when the corridor guards met the ascending detachment.

Sigurd did not understand the words but it all became clear when the booted feet continued up the steps.

"Run, girl," Sigurd ordered.

The spiral of the staircase tightened with no exit in the smooth white walls, save for small slit windows.

"Where does this lead?" He asked.

"I don't know," she pleaded. "I was never here."

They came to a door and raced through it, slamming it behind them and throwing a bolt.

The fugitives found themselves on a narrow wooden platform, bordered by a small railing, atop the turret with the full fury of the storm raging all around them.

They were trapped.

Once again, Sigurd's name was ringing true!

"What do we do now?" Sofia asked. There was apprehension in her voice but no fear. That made Sigurd proud for her.

"Now we fight." He said with a savage joy, then added, "It is too high to jump."

The girl chewed on her lips with concern, thinking deeply for a time then asked, "Do-do you think a Christian can come into Valhalla- to, uh- visit a friend?" It was clear that she was fighting back tears.

Sigurd let his focus stray from the doorway for a moment to look her in the eyes. "Sofia," he said with a warm tone, "Odin would be proud to have a shield maiden like you in his hall." He touched his meaty hand to her tousled hair and patted her head. "And I swear that wherever Christian heaven is I will come and get you personally to bring you to the feast!"

She nodded and sniffled. "I know you will."

"Now," he ordered, "Slam this door behind me and..." he pointed at her knife. "Use that on anyone but me that comes through it." Before she could protest he was though the door and braced his back against it.

Sigurd let a wolfish grin light his features, that had any seen might have thought tinged with madness. *Luckless till the end*, he thought. *A plaything for Loki to give hope to then snatch it away again; but worse to give Sofia hope to let me come this far- to make this escape, only for her to be recaptured. At least there is a chance she will be ransomed by her uncle.* He laughed out loud. "At least I will make them pay dearly for the privilege of her company; that should convince them she is person of great worth!"

The Syrian soldiers were in sight now racing up the steps two abreast, the widest they could be on the narrow stairs.

"Come on you spineless whelps," Sigurd challenged. "I'm sure some of my bad luck will rub off on you!"

The black clad Syrians came on at a fast walk intending to overwhelm the lone Varangian.

Sigurd laughed again and bounded down the five steps to crash into the first of the soldiers. His ferocious unexpected charge unnerved the lead soldiers whom he hacked aside like tall grass, snatching a sword from the dead hand of one of them as he fell into the central well of the staircase.

Now the soldiers behind the first two attempted to halt but the driving pressure of those behind pushed them forward. Sigurd used his double blades to destroy the next two Syrians in a half-dozen strokes.

"Come," the red-haired giant bellowed. "Does the mud of Syria breed anything but drudges and mewling babes?"

The soldiers were finally able to halt, reconsidering their tactical options. They realized they could not advance more than two abreast and there was no way to flank him. It could be a long battle.

Sigurd knew it and laughed again. He moved back up several steps shaking gore from his two blades and waited, breathing easily.

This could take a good while, he thought with humor at the hesitation of the Syrians.

It took the soldiers' commander minutes to browbeat his men from the rear to make them charge again at the insane giant.

Sigurd met the charge as he had the first but with two blades whirling like a thresher of death.

The Syrians were compelled up the steps again by their commander's sword blade, charging into the steel juggernaut again and again where they fell in sprays of gore.

Soon the steps were so slick with blood that the ascending attackers had difficulty finding traction to keep up the attack. They were forced to hurl the bodies of their own men into the central well of the staircase to land below with a sickening thud to enable them to continue their assault.

Sigurd lost track of the number of enemies he hacked as limbs, heads and bodies flew in showers of gore.

He lost track, as well, of the number of wounds he sustained, though none of them of any consequence.

Suddenly, however, there were no more living targets for his flashing blades and he was able to catch his breath.

Below the stairs dripped with the blood, body parts and gore of two dozen men.

"Are there no men in all the south?" Sigurd jeered. When there was no response from below he added, "Then send me boys and dogs; I'm sure they will show better measure than you offal!"

As the red haze of battle faded from the northman he saw why there was a pause; the Syrian commander, tired of losing men, had called in archers.

"Balder's balls!" Sigurd cursed. "Open girl," he called and at the sound of the bolt being thrown open threw himself backward through the door just as a flight of shafts whizzed over him.

The sky was already pink above the observation platform with just a light rain as a reminder of the storm.

Sofia was crouching next to the open door, knife poised to strike any who entered and looked down at him to say, "You're hurt!"

"Bee stings," he said as he sat up to see that the Syrians were again advancing up the stairs, shoving aside their fallen brethren and crouching behind shields.

"This is it, little Freya," He said as he rose. "They have my measure now." He could see the archers beyond the shield men and knew that this rush would be the last.

"Have courage and stay to the side," he said to Sofia.

Hold a place for me this night, Lothar, he thought, *and fill my mead horn full!*

"Odin!" Sigurd yelled as he raised his swords to slice down on the advancing Syrians.

Just then the sky exploded.

A brilliant slash of light brighter than the noonday sun arched from the heavens, danced across both of Sigurd's blades and jumped into the metal shields of the Syrians as they crowded into the doorway.

Sigurd was thrown backward so that he landed partially on the wooden deck and partially on the startled Sofia.

The sky above was suddenly bright blue and cloudless.

It was minutes before the startled two on the platform recovered enough to sit up.

The smell of burnt flesh, ozone and metal was in the air.

"Sofia?" the giant gasped, "are you all right?"

"I-uh- I think so," the girl replied, blinking. "What happen—Sigurd! Your hair, it is white!"

The northman's hair and beard was indeed now all snow white.

"By Thor!" he swore as he looked at his own hair. Then he realized how appropriate an oath it was.

Three times the god of thunder had sent his father's bolts to save Sigurd—once to knock him off the ship so he could live to seek Sofia, once to startle the guard captain and now.

He glanced down the spiral stairs to see that it was littered with charred corpses of the entire Syrian force as well as a sizable chunk of the stairs had been blasted away.

"Now he has slain my enemies," he whispered aloud.

"Look!" Sofia cried as she pointed to the harbor. "The rest of the fleet; the storm must have blown them to us. Praise God, we are saved!"

"Yes," Sigurd smiled. "Praise a god!"

The girl looked up to her hero and giggled. "I shall have to call you Snowbeard the Luckless now."

"No, my little shield maiden," he said, "I am luckless no more; you may call me Sigurd Snowbeard Thorson from this time and forever more!

THE END... FOR NOW.

A few after thoughts on the mythical world of the Vikings...

First things first, there were no people who were actually named 'the Vikings.' Viking is a verb and it means to 'go raiding.' And was what a group of northern European dwelling peoples- Danes, Swedes and Norwegians, who, because of the harsh conditions in their homelands and scarce resources did to survive. They would go raiding and trading in the southern climes to supplement the limited farming times and tough existence at home.

For a long time the world viewed these northern (or Norsemen) as uncultured savages because they, like all tribal cultures, tended to regard the world outside their own group as the enemy and ripe for pickings.

They were, in fact, more egalitarian, less sexist and better educated than most of the peoples they raided. They had a complex social structure and a deeply held set of religious beliefs.

Prior to a mass conversion to Christianity (often at sword point) they worshiped a pantheon of warrior deities.

Prior to this wholesale (and often halfhearted) conversion the religion of the northmen (and women) in the early 1000s was the Astrau. The chief god of many was the All-Father (called variously Woden, Wotan or Odin) from whom we get the day "Wednesday'- for Woden's Day.

This father figure allowed himself to be bound to the world tree in a crucifixion of pain where he suffered to understand the pain of the world and he sacrificed his right eye to gain all seeing knowledge.

He was aided by Loki- the shapeshifting trickster (and father of the Goddess of Death-Hel) and Thor, God of thunder who wielded a magic hammer that returned whenever he threw it. The valkyries were the female gathered of the fallen dead who brought warriors to their reward or to the hall of Odin's wife, Freya.

It was a warrior religion that was part of every aspect of life where lightning, thunder, wind and rain all were the province of specific gods as were crafts, medicine and all skills and trades.

And each of these hearty Norse adventurers, male and female, felt a deep sense of community closely tied with the natural forces all around these seafaring farmers. Nature was an everyday companion and they saw the hand of the gods in everything they did.

The northmen traveled and traded far and wide from Russia (where the country took its name from a tribe of Norse called The Rus) to Africa, India and the North American continents.

In the Mediterranean the Emperor of the Eastern Roman Empire recognized the fierce power, loyalty and fighting skill of such men. The Emperor made Northern born warriors his own personal bodyguards, The Varangian Guard.

Once an oath was sworn on an Oath Ring it was sacred and not even certain death could cause a warrior to break that vow. The Norse warriors believed that death in battle was the highest achievement and that these honored dead rise to a vast eternal feast hall, Valhalla.

To die old or feeble was considered a mark of shame and this is one of the things that drives Sigurd, hero of my story forward.

I hope you enjoy this tale and his further adventures in times to come…

✝✝✝

Teel James Glenn has stories have been printed in magazines from *Weird Tales, Spinetingler, SciFan, Mad, Black Belt, Fantasy Tales, Pulp Empire, Sherlock Holmes Mystery, SciFan, Sixgun Western, Crimson Streets, Silver Blade Quarterly, Tales of Old, Blazing Adventures* and scores of other publications and dozens of books and anthologies in many genres. His short story "The Clockwork Nutcracker" won best steampunk story for 2013 from Preditor and Editors poll. His novel *A Cowboy in Carpathia: A Bob Howard Adventure* won Best Novel 2021 in the Pulp Factory Award. He is also the winner of the 2012 Pulp Ark Award for Best Author. He was a finalist for the Derringer Short Mystery Award in 2022. His novel, *Callback for a Corpse*, was a second-place winner in the CWR Poll as best mystery.

Teel's website is: TheUrbanSwashbuckler.com

HERCULES AND THE WRATH OF THE RED SORCERESS

BY ELIZABETH FREEMAN

Anansi's web covered the world, its miniscule, invisible strands crossing continents so that he could gather stories and tales Stories of love, stories of hope, tales of sorrow, tales of joy, he read them all and shared them with the world. But as the sounds of battle rang out in the celestial halls, he had little time as he struggled to find the right leads. The first part of his plan was already in motion, the dark-skinned sorceress clad in red stood before him her eyes glowing crimson.

"Who are you? Where are the rest of the Orisha?" she asked picking him up by the collar of his shirt. "Anansi, the God of stories," a lopsided grin came to his face.

The Red Sorceress let out a deep, cold laugh. "I have no need for your worthless powers," she said tossing him to the ground. The phrase repeated itself in Anansi's brain. Worthless? he had given mankind stories and yet he was deemed worthless. He looked upon his grand web, a plan starting to take shape. Spider legs burst from his back, letting him manipulate the web in more fine detail. So far, the story was in its infancy but now all it took was making the right connections.

☩☩☩

The boat pitched and rolled through the storm, as Hercules griped the bow as if daring the God's of this strange land to strike him down. Athena had come to him in a dream, clothed in golden armor with her spear in her right hand.

"Son of Zeus! Find the Daughter of Lightening in the heart of Aethiopia and bring forth the storm to slay the Red Sorceress."

"Red Sorceress? I've slain the Nemean lion, routed rivers, and fought amazons what do I have to fear from a simple sorceress?" Hercules asked.

The goddess's stern face scolded. "Prideful as always. This Sorceresses power is older than the Titans. Even Chronos feared it. He devoured us to gain enough power to stand against it, but the power vanished before he could challenge it. Now it has returned."

Althoughin a dream, that made Hercules pause. The titans had nearly defeated the Gods once before and Chronos had taken a triumvirate of Zeus, Poseidon, and Hades to stop. For this entity to be even stronger than them was a cause for concern. He bolted awake just as the sun's warming rays had come through his window. He heard panicked screams. Instinctively he grabbed his sword and shield only to find human sized dogs in the streets. He'd never seen such beasts before. One of the dark brown, furred spotted creatures with a small snout and long legs ran after a young boy, his short legs making him easy prey. As the strange beasts' jaws widened to snap at the child the Son of Zeus jumped in front of him. A pained laughing sound erupted from the creature's throat as it hit the enchanted bronze shield which Hercules swung in front of him with all his might. The beast was hurled into a stone pillar which cracked and crumbled, pinning the creature under it.

The three-remaining dog-like creatures turned their attention to Hercules, while the rest of the crowd fled.

"That's right you overgrown hounds, eyes on me," he muttered his sword at the ready. For such large creatures they were supernaturally fast. In the span of two heart beats, two of them circled him, saliva dripping from their mouths as their strange laughter vibrated in his ears. Hercules dodged a bite from the creature before him, only to cry out as claws ran down his back.

'*They're far smarter than they look.*' he thought as he gripped the creature on his back by the scruff of its neck hurling it into its partner. Yips of pain came from both attackers as the crunch of bone followed. The Son of Zeus stabbed them both with his sword. That left only one. The final creature was wary, having learnt from its fallen comrades. They kept their distance, black eyes locked on Hercules. Blood dripped from the creature's muzzle as it crushed a man's lifeless body under its paws.

Guilt made Hercules strike first, sword reflecting the sun's rays into the beast's eyes temporarily blinding his foe. That spilt second gave the Son of Zeus the moment he needed. But the beast was just as sly, side stepping a blow that would sever its head clean from its body. Fangs bit into the shield, although enchanted the bronze dented from the sheer strength of the jaws. Hercules stabbed the beast's underbelly just as the razor-sharp fangs pierced the shield held only a few centimeters away from his head. The agony made the large dog release the shield as the sword ran the creature straight through.

Splattered in blood and shaking with adrenaline Hercules took a few deep breaths to let his battle rage subside. Bodies lay scattered across the cobble-stone streets. Men, women, even a child laid battered and bloody. With his great strength, he couldn't save everyone. The survivors came out of hiding, some to collect and mourn the dead others to cheer and praise their savior.

Hercules wiped his sword on the beast's fur. "Where did these creatures come from?" he asked.

"I've seen their ilk in Aethiopia" a merchant cried, popping out from behind his spice stall. "The locals call them Hyenas, but I've never seen them that big before, let alone attacking people unprovoked."

Aethiopia, Athena had mentioned that far off land in his dream. Looks like these creatures were added incentive.

"Merchant, where's the nearest ship that I can take to this Aethiopia?" he asked. With no time to waste, he packed food, his sword and shield, draped himself in the Nemean lion cloak, having learned from this encounter to watch his back. He said a quick prayer for the souls of the dead and another to Athena for wisdom in the battles ahead.

✝✝✝

Finding a captain that was willing go to Aethiopia, especially after news of the hyena attack had spread, was difficult. Most took it as a sign from the gods to stay away from the land.

"Name's Zosimos, Captain of the *Golden Deer*. Heard you've been looking for a boat to Aethiopia. I'm your man" the short man with leaf green eyes said while leaning against the door to the bar where Hercules had been asking around.

"How much do you charge?" He asked following Zosimos to his boat. "Depends on where you're heading to."

"That is the question, my friend. All I know is that it's somewhere in Aethiopia. Athena was rather vague," he admitted.

"How about we just head to Thebes for now? A city that big should have whatever you're looking for" Zosimos said presenting his small, nimble cargo ship with a single mast.

To give Captain Zosimos extra incentive he gave him five decadrachm, each worth ten drachmae each. Zosimos's eyes widened larger than the coins. "Hoist the main sail, you lot. We've got a passenger!"

At first, the *Golden Deer* made great time sailing out of Athens by noon, her hull full of Greek pottery, wine and animals hides for trade. But by the fifth day at sea the weather had taken a turn. The once calm, tranquil waters stirred into waves thanks to black storm clouds that had rolled in from the Aegean.

The helmsmen struggled to keep her steady, but the wind and blinding rain tossed the boat about like it was toy. From the smashing sounds in the hull, some of the pottery wasn't going to survive the trip.

"The storms too fierce! We'll drown!" Captain Zosimos cried as a wave swept over the deck taking a pair of sailors with it as they tried to keep the sail from tearing in the wind.

Hercules could sense that this far from home, his father's power was weaker. Calling on him would do little good. There was a snap as the mast started to fall. Without a second thought, the demigod gripped the tree trunk sized mast with all his strength, fighting the forces of nature, to keep it up right.

"Tie it to me!" he yelled over the roar of the storm. Those few sailors that did hear him obeyed, battling the elements while tying the mast to him so that he made the sail stand tall. Sharp, salty winds cut at his skin, waves threatened to drown him filling his lungs with water only to recede and return once more. His eyes stung from the salt, yet still he stood.

The rest of the crew had done the sane thing; fleeing below decks, save for the valiant helmsmen who strained to keep the *Golden Deer* steady and the captain who refused to abandon his post.

For a moment, through the dark clouds, a man danced in a skirt of crimson which twirled in time with his steps. The booms of thunder became drumbeats, and the flashes of lightening revealed a god that seemed to be chiseled from pure obsidian, his brown eyes glowed with blue sparks as he danced faster and faster in time with storm.

"Like my welcome gift, little one?" The god's voice was sweet as honey but there was an edge to it like the tip of a sword.

"It's quite spectacular!" Hercules called out as the thunder stopped and the storm ceased as if it had never been.

"The Red Sorceress will test you far more then I have. That's why I, Shango, King of Thunder and Lightning, am sending you aid."

Shango's bare feet sounded like booming thunder as he walked on deck. "You'll need this to find her." The God of Thunder and Lightning handed the Son of Zeus a simple bronze compass. "Follow it and you will find my daughter." With that the god disappeared in a flash of lightening and with him the rain petered out in a heartbeat. Hercules held the bronze compass which pointed due south.

The ship sailed down the Nile for days, passed the white Pyramids capped with gold. Children raced after the boat along the docks, waving and laughing. Hercules waved back, but still the compass pushed him further south. They stopped at mighty Thebes, so the captain could unload his cargo and get yelled at by irate Greek merchants whose precious pottery was now reduced to shards, thanks to the storm. While they spent a week being docked and fitted with a new mast, Hercules loitered around in taverns and markets, eyeing his bronze compass. Yet instead of pointing to the packed to bursting city, it pointed towards the Nile and bade him to go deeper down the river still.

The land along the riverbank gradually changed from fertile, irrigated farmland to rocky, uneven terrain.

"We're passing the First Cataract now" Captain Zosimos said as the Nile narrowed. "These natural narrow bends in the river are called Cataracts. This one marks that we are now out of Egyptian territory and into Nubian land" he explained to Hercules, clearly prideful to impart to his wealth of knowledge to his captive audience. With the ease borne from years of sailing the captain guided the ship through the rocky, whitewater rapids expertly dodging rocks that jutted out from the riverbed. The Nile seemed endless as farmland battled against rocky mountains and barren desert for space. Dark skinned farmers were too hard at work to notice or care about one of hundreds of ships that sailed down this trade heavy waterway that bore a living legend. Although a few did smile his way, not because of who he was but simply to be friendly.

The strange compass didn't stop pointing south as they passed trade hubs like Kerma, near the third Cataract. Some of the men began to whisper that this quest was a fool's errand. Trying to find one person in a kingdom with millions of inhabitants? Perhaps these foreign gods were up to strange tricks. A glance from Hercules as he stood at the bow silenced any descent. Every Greek knew tales of the Son of Zeus's powerful rage and did not want to witness it firsthand.

But seasoned Captain Zosimos stayed the course. Having seen Shango firsthand doubt was far from his mind. He'd sailed this route dozens of time trading for ivory, gold, and even strange beasts like the long-necked creature known as a giraffe or even a baby elephant. Wealthy Greeks would pay a pretty drachma for such goods.

After days of traveling in peace as passed, they passed the Fourth Cataract, the mud brick walls of Napata, the capital of Nubia, came into view. The formerly stationary compass pointed to city with unwavering certainty.

✝✝✝

Hercules paid Zosimos and his crew extra for repairs, to make up for the week he'd cost them in Thebes as well for taking him much farther than they expected.

"May you find the person you're searching for, Hercules," Captain Zosimos said as the famed hero disembarked. The docks were a hive of activity. Burnoose wearing traders leading their camels haggled for goods next to a Persian man who twirled his fine mustache at the astronomical prices. A Spartan, his golden shield polished to a shine, laughed at the joke of a Nubian as they clinked goblets together. Farmers brought their herds of cows and sheep to market guiding them with their crooked staffs into pens. Vendors hawked their wares crying in a myriad of languages, only a few of which Hercules recognized. Mud brick buildings, of all shapes and sizes, sprang up from the docks, and led deeper into the city. Labored groans could be heard from giant warehouses, where sailors carried heavy sacks grain to and fro while a female scribe kept meticulous records. Hercules passed buildings with wooden doors carved with intricate figures of humans and animals like crocodiles, and turtles. Most interestingly, no one gave him the time of day. Unlike Thebes, Athens or even Sparta where people would cry praises, men and women would throw themselves at him seeking to hear tales of his legendary deeds while some wanted more carnal pleasures which he eagerly obliged, here he was just another foreigner most likely here to do business. There was something pleasant about being able to lose oneself in a crowd. Of not having the endless expectations to be great and noble all the time, but even with the air of business, underneath it all there was a sense of wariness as if at any moment the normalcy could be shattered. Umber skinned men and women armed with spears and shields others with swords patrolled the streets. Although he wasn't a native, he could tell from the tension in the air that this was abnormal. As he walked from the docks, the street covered by architectural triangular archways narrowed. Shango's compass pointed him down a side street, deeper into Napata. Towering above the city was a seventy-meter tall mountain he'd heard the natives call Jebel Barkal, whose shade he was grateful for as the sun's piercing heat beat down on him. According to the compass he was getting closer to Shango's Daughter.

A chill went down his spine, as if he'd been plunged down a well. Something was wrong. Hercules ran down the street pushing his way past citizens, merchants and street performers until the street opened out into a main square. At first everything seemed normal, but it all changed when the strange purple mist rolled in. A deep belly laugh came from the cloth stall at the end of the street. The woman behind the counter couldn't stop laughing, her eyes going from happy to panicked and then the transformation began. She fell to her knees her laughter became an agonizing scream as brown, spotted fur sprouted from her skin and her bones painfully reknit themselves transforming into a bestial monster. The shop owner tried tried to utter a plea for help, but only guttural sounds erupted from her throat as the transformation continued while the crowd looked on in horror. Her nails grew into three-inch long talons as her face slowly deformed and lengthened to become a dog like snout. A stubby tail burst forth as she rose to her paw like feet. As the spell took hold of her mind the fear that had enveloped her was now long forgotten.

"Kill the Children of the Storm," she snarled hungrily. Slowly the twisted hyena-like laughter infected the crowd, as the mist wove its way throughout the market, latching on young and old alike. Hercules watched in horror as some of market shoppers were transformed into were-hyenas, their haunting laughter echoing all around him. The Son of Zeus drew his sword, his hands shook as the smallest of the hyena beasts pounced aiming for his jugular. He'd seen his attacker before, a child who only moments before were begging his mother for a drink of coconut water. Yet now, he was reduced to a growling, blood thirsty beast. Seeing no other option, Hercules's mighty punch sent the creature flying into one of the stalls, smashing it to pieces. The few soldiers that hadn't been infected struggled against the tide of beasts. For each one they took down, two more took their place. The compass swung behind Hercules as a black arrow whizzed passed his ear striking the hyena beast that was sneaking up on him. As Hercules fists sent creatures flying, the mysterious archer's arrows rained down pain with a precision that would make a Spartan weep with joy. Soon the attackers were down to three. Two strong beasts jumped Hercules pinning him as the third, the former clothing stall owner, escaped towards the rolling dunes of the desert. The black arrows were no match for her supernatural speed.

Hercules elbowed both of his attackers in the chest so hard that he heard the crack of ribs. The sudden pain caused the creatures to let go as black arrows blossomed in their shoulders sending them down for the count.

"So, you're the Son of Thunder, eh. I thought you'd be taller?" A dark-skinned woman with a runner's sleek, strong built jumped gracefully down from the roof top of a nearby building. She crossed her muscular arms as she put away her long bow, looking Hercules up and down as if he were a pig at market. She had her father's dark skin tone; an obsidian hue that made Hercules think of the space between the stars. She had three ritual scarification marks on each cheek. The striking facial markings immediately set her apart from her Nubian counterparts, that, and her eyes which were the color of the purest gold. Her large dreadlocks, as thick as her arms, were done in one braid that reached the center of her back and covered her quiver brimmed with black arrows with white fletching. A pair of curved blades hung from her hips. The curve was so deep that it formed a crescent moon shape, but it was her leopard pelt cape that caught his attention. The beast's fur was sunbeam yellow, its spots blacker than night. The leopards face was trapped in an eternal snarl which now formed its hood. In contrast, her leather armor with a studded skirt and sandals came off as plain.

"Thank you for the help…"

"General Ojo! What do we do with the surviving Bouda?" A lanky soldier with umber skin asked, his shoulder scarred by a deep wound. Hercules had lost count after twenty-five at the number of troops in the streets before the attack now only a hand full remained. The corpses of sheep and cattle were scattered about, easy prey for the Bouda. The once busy market looked like the inside of a slaughterhouse with bodies of human and animal mixed as crimson seeped into the cobble stones.

"Lieutenant Tabid, see that your wound is tended to. Tell the others to get treated as well," she replied and then turned to Hercules.

"I am Abeni Ojo, General of Queen Unatti. My father, Shango, sent me a dream which told me to meet you here. Help my troops to tie up the Bouda."

"In my experience, Gods tend to be rather…selective in the information they tell their progeny," Hercules replied, choosing his words carefully. Although he was an ocean away from Greece, he dared not anger his father he thought as he grabbed a coil of rope from the now ruined stall. Along with the troops they made quick work of the unconscious citizens tying them together in small groups.

"When did all this start?" Hercules asked as he pulled the rope tighter around a pack of were-beasts.

"About ten days ago, I'd heard rumors about a strange fog coming from somewhere in the jungles to the south of Napata, past the desert. Any animal that met the strange mist became violent, even docile camels turned on their masters trampling them to death. At first I thought it was nothing more than hearsay but then the Ambassadors caravan was late." Abeni paused, her golden orbs haunted as she headed for the city walls. "Report back to the barracks. Hercules and I will track down the remaining Bouda." Although some were injured, the remaining soldiers saluted proudly and obeyed her orders unquestioningly. After her troops left, she continued her tale.

"All thirty members of the caravan had been transformed into were-beasts. I tried to reason with them, but they kept muttering about 'Killing the Daughter of the Storm', so I slew them before they had a chance to enter the city."

"There are tracks here. We can find our runaway," she pointed to faint indentations in the sand that hadn't yet been blown away by the whipping winds. The Bouda ignored the well-worn road that led to the city. The dunes seemed to roll on endlessly as Abeni led the way. The sun's blindingly hot rays beat down on the Son of Zeus, his skin burning. His throat dried up after half an hour of walking. Abeni tossed him her water skin which he drunk greedily, taking all his willpower to not drain it dry. As he returned it to his fellow demigod, she continued her tale.

"Ambassador Nabra was a dear friend of mine. She treated me like a sister when others saw me as an outsider from a distant land. Yet, when I found her amongst the wreckage of the caravan, she tried to rip my throat out. The only mercy I could give her was to send her to the afterlife as painlessly as possible. So, for her sake, I'll find a cure so no more people will suffer." Abeni's hushed tones reached Hercules ears as they came to an oasis. The Daughter of Shango clicked her tongue. Hercules could make out dozens of tracks of all shapes and sizes. This was a popular watering hole making it impossible to tell where the transformed woman had fled.

Abeni whistled and a messenger hawk flew down from the branches. It must have been following them for miles. She took out the piece of paper the creature had been carrying in a message tube on its back and scanned the note. From her belt pouch she withdrew a writing implement and wrote a hasty reply. "My troops have escorted the surviving Bouda to prison for their own safety. I told them to leave us horses at the city gate, I am to formally introduce you to the Queen Unatti, she's been expecting you."

✝✝✝

"What news do you bring, servant?" The Red Sorceress snapped as the newly turned Bouda bowed before her. The entire land would soon pay her the respect she rightfully deserved. After all, they had shunned her, banished her to the desert like a dog, now they would suffer.

"The Daughter of the Storm and the Son of Lightening have met. They defeated our forces."

Even the advanced forces she'd sent by transforming those Egyptian merchants had been defeated. It seemed the stories about the prowess of Hercules were more than simple tales spouted by prideful Greeks, some who even worshiped him as a god.

"No matter, I can always make more," she said as she eyed a sleepy little village nestled at the foot of the hill on which she stood. Children played while women gossiped at the well, laughing and chatting. Older teens worked the sorghum fields. For a moment she felt a memory bubbled up inside her. Her mother humming softly as she hemmed a skirt. As a little girl, Winji had found some cloth scraps and copied her mother's stitches.

"Look! My doll has a skirt now," Winji cried with pride. Her mother looked down and smiled. It had been so long ago that the memory of her own moth-

...HAWK FLEW DOWN FROM THE BRANCHES.

er's face was hazy, focusing on their identical sliver eyes, the feeling of her tender hugs and half remembered lullaby's.

"My little star will be a seamstress in no time!" Her mother put down her work hugging her daughter.

It was time to introduce herself to her new puppets. She went down alone, her forces hiding in the tall grass. The children immediately gathered around her.

"Where are you from?"

"Your cloak is pretty!"

"Do you want to play Hounds and Jackals?"

A tan skinned woman at the well looked up. "Don't you have chores to do? The sorghum isn't going to pick itself, is it now?" The children ran off, waving at Winji as they went to work.

"Excuse their nosiness. We only get a few travelers usually stopping from caravans although even those have been scarce lately. I'm Sela, it's almost lunch would you care to share with us?"

Winji gave a warm smile. "That would be lovely Sela. I haven't had a good meal in days now." That wasn't a lie. Sacking villages and growing her army left little time for meals. In truth, she had forgotten the last time she'd eaten. The scent of fresh baked bread filled the air as Sela pulled out a pair of buns from the oven. Goat stew shimmered over the fireplace. The home maker piled her guest's plate high with stew and bread. Winji ate ignoring that the food tasted like ash on her tongue or that bread felt like sandpaper against her insides. She could sense that her forces had the small village surrounded, the Bouda awaiting her mental command.

'*How many in the village?*' the Red Sorceress asked telepathically.

'*Twelve, Mistress. All hardy and strong.*' the Bouda from the capital replied.

"That was wonderful! You're a gifted cook. I haven't tasted anything this lovely even in the capital." The lies rolled easily off the sorceress tongue as she mentally ordered the attack in the same breath.

Sela gave a shy smile, tucking her hair behind her ear. "It's just an old family recipe, nothing that compares to the capital. Would you like to stay the night? We don't have much, but my husband and I would love your company."

"Thank you for the kind offer but I won't be able to take you up on it. I have a pair of friends to visit by nightfall" she replied as Sela poured her a cup of water.

Screams came from the fields. Sela turned suddenly, dropping her pitcher, and making a mad dash towards her children's pained voices. Winji followed with fake fear plastered on her face. Chaos erupted all around them as the miasma seeped across the sorghum field. In such a small town the spell took hold much faster turning simple farmers into wild dogs, eager for their Mistresses's orders. The shattering of farm of tools, smashed pottery and burned food filled the air as panic swept across the village.

Sela started to sob trembling as she watched the last light of humanity fade from her children's eyes as the spell took hold. "The meal was lovely. Let me reward you for your kindness." Winji said coldly.

"Why? Why would you do this? We…we welcomed you with open arms?" she choked out in confusion.

Winji cocked her head to one side as if trying to remember what emotion she was supposed to feel. Guilt? Sadness? Some other feeling she'd long forgotten the words for.

"Because your village was here" she replied wiping away Sela's panicked tears with the back of her hand.

The purple miasma racked Sela's body with agony, muscles and bones contorting into unnatural shapes. Winji looked on, ignoring the flames and blood shed as Sela became a lioness who towered over the Red Sorceress. The once loving mother ignored the creatures that had once been her own children even their names forgotten as only Winji's will mattered now.

"Arise my bodyguard, we have much to do."

Queen Unatti's palace was a sight to behold, twin pyramids reached into the heavens and the gigantic carved, stone gates greeted them. As soon as the guardswoman on duty caught sight of General Ojo she signaled to her companion. The gates swung open welcomingly and a stable hand waited to take their horses.

As she dismounted, General Ojo instructed the servant to send a messenger to Queen Unatti that she had found the Son of Lightening. The servant bowed and rushed into the torch lit halls. The demigods' footsteps echoed on the marble floors as they approached the Queen's welcoming chambers.

"I heard what happened in Napata. My prison now overruns with my own people. General, do you have any leads on what foul magic is causing this?" the Queen asked. She was as dark as Abeni but only reached up to the demigoddess's waist at a small 4'5 height. Her hair was done up in a well-kept afro, a circlet of gold rested on her forehead and her robes were of the finest snow-white cotton. Although she was a queen, she adorned herself modestly with golden arm bands and choker. Her brown eyes locked on the General who then dropped on one knee.

"Forgive me, my Queen. I managed to follow one of the turned ones but lost them in the desert. The only good news I have to report is that I bring with me the one known as Hercules, the Son of Zeus."

The Queen looked Hercules up and down. "This is the man the Gods said would aid you in defeating the sorceress. What can he do?"

"Zeus has gifted me with strength that rivals any man. I have diverted rivers, fought Amazons armies and sailed with Jason and his Argonauts."

"You have strength but what of wisdom? General, show him what I mean" Queen Unatti stated incredulously, prompting Abeni to challenge the Son of Zeus.

"None may wield weapons in front of the Queen," the servant who'd guided them to the hall ordered. Hercules flexed his muscles as he handed his weapons to the servant who struggled to carry them. He wondered what the General would do. He could easily crush her like an ant. The general shrugged off his swift jabs, something not even Hippolyta had done.

"I am blessed by Shango. You'll have to do more than that," she chided dodging blows with uncanny speed. It was as if she was the wind itself. Every time he thought he'd had her, she shifted. Then her fist hit him in the face. It was more than just a simple punch. The blow came with electricity that was focused only on him, his muscles spasmed as he was flung into a brazier on the wall. Embers fell at his feet as he wiped blood from his lip.

The General's body was coated in a layer of electricity, her golden orbs glowing like twin suns. "Shango is the God of storms and thunder. Like my father, I am not one to be underestimated." A powerful gust of wind thrusted him into the ceiling. As he fell, the General waved her arm creating a cushion of air that put him gingerly back on his feet, all while she had a prideful grin on her face.

Anger started to cloud his vision. Beaten by a foreign warrior woman and embarrassed in front of a Queen! He was Hercules! Son of Zeus! Champion of the Gods! Holding back was the last thing on his mind now. He would show this so called "General" what true strength was! He charged, anger letting him push through the winds. He gave a cocky laugh as his right hook connected with Abeni's face, there was familiar crunch of cartilage as her nose broke. The follow up blow went for her stomach but a wall of electricity that felt thicker than a bronze shield met his fist. Abeni kicked him, sending him down on one knee. He grabbed her waist as he fell, and both tumbled to the floor.

"Stop!" Both fighters startled by the Queen's command froze in their tracks. A small crowd of servants had gathered, as did a few soldiers brought by the earth-shaking force of their attacks. The throne room was a mess, the wall mural had a huge chunk missing; the ceiling had a body shaped imprint on it. But Hercules eyes were focused on something else entirely. Up close, Abeni's scars were beautiful and the fierceness in her eyes was captivating, but her face was an unreadable mask. The demigods got to their feet both glaring at each other.

"Hercules, I cannot tell if your presence here is a blessing or some divine trial to test me in this trying time. At first light both of you, along with a contingent of troops, will search for the source of this magic. Just don't kill each other," the Queen ordered.

"Can I break his nose? Technically that's not lethal." Abeni asked, crimson dripping down her nose.

"You can try," Hercules scoffed, his wounded pride not letting him back down. "If I could use weapons, it would be a different story."

"Oh, so you need mortal tools to be effective. Any soldier can be good with a blade. All you've got is a head full of rocks and muscles the size of a camel's hump" Abeni chided.

"Enough! Take Hercules to the guest chambers for the evening and send a doctor to both him and the General." The Queen rubbed her temples, wondering why demigods were so hot blooded.

Both demigod's bowed, Hercules followed a wide-eyed servant girl out while Abeni headed in the opposite direction surrounded by her troops who spoke in a language Hercules didn't understand. From the chorus of laughter that echoed down the hall, he guessed she was mocking him as if he were some common mercenary and not a demigod. He clutched his fist as he headed to his quarters. Bits of rock and plaster fell from his short brown hair some even clung to his close-cropped beard.

✝✝✝

Abeni didn't suffer fools. Out of all the children of Gods, the Orisha had chosen a muscular idiot. It made her miss Yorubaland even more. But Shango himself had appeared before her. He'd floated down from the sky on a gale, his twin axes glowing with power, his bare chest muscled. She had her father's dark obsidian skin and dada hair that naturally formed dreadlocks.

"Evil stirs in the heart of Nubia. Go, my daughter. The son of Lightening will be your aid." When she'd returned home and told her mother she would have to leave it was then that she had received the leopard skinned cloak which she cherished dearly. That's how she'd found herself a General for a foreign Queen in the heart of Nubia. The thought helped her ignore the mild annoyance of her nose being set by the physician. Although, it had been fun to have a bout where she didn't need to hold back as much in a fight. When she sparred with others, she often held back out fear of accidently hurting a comrade in arms. She'd once broken a man's arm with a haymaker during training after getting so lost in the rhythm of the fight.

Tomorrow, she would show the Greek what respect really meant.

✝✝✝

Abeni was up before the first rays of dawn touched the sky. After washing up, she put on her amor and sheathed her blades. Lastly, she shouldered the saddle bags which she'd packed the night before. The daughter of Shango walked into the training yard to find Hercules already up and training with a wooden practice dummy. His sword swings were controlled, focused and confident. His short brown hair was damp with sweat, meaning he'd been up even earlier than her. His storm grey eyes were focused on his foe.

"Not bad" Abeni said pointing him in the direction of the stables. The Grecian demigod followed picking up his worn saddle bags on his broad shoulders.

"About yesterday…" he said, rubbing the back of his neck with his free hand.

"We both got carried away. It's not every day one gets to challenge a fellow demigod" she replied. "Although if we'd kept going, I would have won," she added playfully as the stable hand brought out their horses. One was a dirt brown mare with bright, inquisitive eyes and the other was a dapple grey stallion with a calm demeanor.

Abeni mounted the dapple-grey stallion with practiced ease, Hercules followed suit with the brown mare. Ten mounted troops with bows and quivers full of arrows strapped to their backs, and even more clipped on to their saddles, awaited them in the courtyard of the palace. The men and women were dressed for war in leather breastplates and animal skinned skirts. Hercules had heard of the accuracy and skill of Nubian archers from Egyptians in Thebes who feared them.

"Move out!" General Ojo commanded. They moved in two columns one behind the General and the others following Hercules. They traveled in formation from the palace to Napata. As they entered through the main gate, the city was a buzz of activity. From how packed the market was, it was as if yesterday's attack was a distant memory, but the stains of dried blood on the walls of some buildings as well as between the cobblestones, stalls that had been hastily patched with rope and had their canvas resewn with different fabric, and there was a grim air about the place. Even this early there were a few vendors whose cries for sales felt muted and the enthusiasm of the early morning shoppers was more hurried, as if they didn't want to spend much time in the place where so much blood had been spilt the day before.

The crowds made way for General Ojo and her troops. "Did the foreigners cause this curse?" a voice in the crowd muttered in a horse whisper. "After all the General is from Yorubaland and the olive-skinned stranger comes from across the ocean," said another woman.

"You forget that's the General who saved us from those pirates a few months back, or how she cleared the trade routes of desert bandits so your goods could get to Cairo, Amaros" she pointed to the man who'd started the fuss about foreigners in the first place. "And Hula, didn't you tell me you found them both attractive yesterday. Or have your tastes changed overnight?" Hula blushed redder than a tomato and looked down at her feet, ashamed. The brave woman continued. "She's saved us more times than I can count. Now, Shush!" The woman's voice erupted louder than the crowd's murmured dissent. The muttered voices turned positive focusing on how skilled her batch of troops were, how kind Abeni was to shop keepers and how that olive skinned foreigner had aided in defense of the city the day before.

"They're so quick to turn on us," Hercules said as they left the city walls far behind them. "They speak out of fear. Some lost loved ones yesterday while others have always found me strange," electricity crackled around her braids as she gave a heavy sigh, the sparks fading. "All they want is to be safe from this magic and that's something I know we can handle."

"My power may not be as flashy as your bolts, but I'm glad to lend a hand," Hercules added which made Abeni roll her eyes. The horses galloped across the dunes kicking up sand and dust in their wake making good time across the sweltering sands. By the time the sun reached its zenith the travelers were on the way to Meroe, following the caravan routes. Even the horses had started to slow their gait, growing weary.

"C'mon gal, almost there. Just a little longer," he encouraged riding up to Abeni as she looked at her map.

"This route is usually heavy with Saharan nomadic traders, but if even they are avoiding it, something is wrong. The curse must be spreading faster than we expected," she said nervously. They rode till night fall, making a small camp in the middle of the endless expanse. Hercules had heard that desert nights were cold; he had to wrap the lions' fur around himself to keep away the biting chill. During the day he kept the lion pelt in his saddle bag lest he sweat like a roast pig on a spit. He helped set up tents while Abeni lit a small fire. Tabid handed Hercules a piece of jerky which the Grecian gladly accepted. They ate jerky and drank water, huddling around the fire for warmth.

"This place has a truly unique beauty to it," Hercules said. "Even if the sun has a personal vendetta against you?" Abeni asked. Hercules laughed "Yes, maybe that's the case."

"This land has bewitched me as well. There's something about the way the dunes roll and the kindness of the people. You'd think in a land this harsh people would hoard what they have using survival as an excuse, but it's the opposite. It's nothing like the jungles of my homeland or the grand city of Ile-Ife, but I think that's why it holds a special place in my heart," Hercules hadn't expected the General to be so candid with him or her troops. But, apparently her candor made the troops relax Some took bets on a game of dice which was something Hercules could understand even with the language barrier, while a pair of soldiers played a small board game of Hounds and Jackels all while Abeni took first watch. She pulled her leopard skin around herself, becoming a giant leopard and began to patrol the edges of the camp. The Son of Zeus expected some cry of shock or fear, but they were too engrossed in their moments of relaxation that they didn't care, or they'd seen her do this before.

Hercules decided to join in the dice game and a short bubbly woman introduced herself.

"I'm Shira."

"My sister's real name is the Queen of Luck" the man next to her said. He had her same small nose and green eyes.

"Kinya, don't scare him off. I'm saving up for a pair of oxen" she said playfully in flawless Greek.

"I've got a bit of luck myself" Hercules replied sitting down next to them. No matter the country or language the rolling of dice and the sound of betting is universally enthralling.

"Our parents are merchants, so we had to pick up languages pretty quickly. The game's Odds or Evens."

Kinya placed the dice on a small woven mat letting the gamblers examine them before the game began. This pair was made of bone painted with Greek numerical symbols. Hercules smiled at least he had a chance. Kinya placed them in a wooden cup and shook.

"Remember the rules you can't bet more than ten bronze. The general doesn't want us wasting all our pay" Shira reminded.

"I bet five bronze on odds" Hercules cried.

"I bet ten bronze on evens" Shira yelled.

The dice rolled out of the cup landing on a double six totaling twelve. Shira laughed. "Pay up!" The other players tossed her bronze coins while Hercules added five drachma to her winnings. Perhaps the luck of the gods was with him, as he won two later rounds of dice giving him a handful of bronze coins. General Ojo, still in her leopardess form, strolled up to the fire, her troops nodding in acknowledgment as their games came to an end. Shira scooped her

"THE GAME IS ODDS AND EVEN."

winnings gleefully, winking at Hercules.

"Kinya, weren't you going to help me with my tent?" she asked her brother.

"Your tent's fine."

"No, I think it's got a hole that needs fixing right now," she muttered, dragging him away. Hercules chuckled. The demigods sat in companionable silence around the crackling flames.

"Is that one of your father's gifts?" Hercules asked.

"No, it's from my mother, Folade. Her people are skilled hunters and huntresses blessed with the ability to become a chosen beast by wearing its skin. While my magics come from my father, my prowess as a warrior is from my mother's love and training," she said gazing up at the stars longingly thinking of home and wondering what her mother was doing at this very moment.

"Your mother must be quite proud. I've run into very few warriors as skilled in both combat and command as you" Hercules said.

Abeni's laugh sounded like a deep roar. "Now I know you're worn out for you're quite quick to flatter me. Forgive me for the other night; I was rude to you while you are a guest in this land. I know you Greeks values hospitality."

"No need to apologize General, sparring with you was quite enjoyable. I hope to get a chance to do it again sometime."

"Perhaps once this chaos is over, I would gladly take you on any day" Abeni said her taunting air coming across in her eyes.

"I'll take next watch" Hercules said trying to smother a loud yawn. She gave a small nod of thanks, taking human form once more with a lazy, cat like stretch. "Wake me if so much as a hair is out of place."

"Yes, General!" he snapped to attention. Too tired to play along she just walked to her tent, waving, and joking with her troops as she passed. He pulled the lions fur tighter. At least he could see the stars. Above his head the sky was bejeweled with thousands of twinkling stars. He could make out Orion and Taurus charting their way across the heavens reminding him that his home was now hundreds of miles and an ocean away. The crackle from the fire and the chatter of the archers kept him up as he scanned the horizon. It was still, save a few animal calls that he couldn't recognize and therefore couldn't tell if they were out of place or not, but he didn't get the same pit of dread feeling that he'd gotten in the market or in Athens. They were safe for now at least.

Suddenly the cold desert night went quiet, the stirring of animals, even the soft night breeze stilled.

"We've got trouble!" Hercules yelled, but only General Ojo raced from her tent while tightening the straps on her armor and drawing her swords.

"Rally around me now!" the general ordered but not a soul stirred. The dying camp fire sprang to life with unnatural purple flames casting an eerie glow about the place.

"Let them rest. They've had a long day after all" said a woman, who because of her crimson cloak must have been the Red Sorceress. At her side was a seven-foot tall lioness woman, arms crossed over her large bust, her talons ready to kill at her mistress' command. A pack of eleven transformed people in the form of bipedal wild dogs stood behind them. With spotted fur, big ears, and long snouts they looked less intimidating than the Bouda, but from the sheer numbers they posed a threat.

"I come to you not as an enemy but as a friend."

"A friend who slaughters innocent people!" Abeni spat.

"You possess great power, but you restrain yourself needlessly. If you wished, you could call down a thunderstorm right now, but you don't?"

"Because that would be a waste of power and draw unnecessary attention" Abeni replied.

"You're a demigod. The blood of Shango flows through your veins yet you fear the ridicule of mortals who you could easily crush" the Red sorceress enquired.

"She's not a heartless murderer like you!" Hercules snapped.

"Ahh, Alcaeus. The man who fears Hera so much that he changed his name to appease her. You of all people know what it's like to have innocent blood on your hands for example Creotiades, and your other seven sons." She paused, her silver eyes gleaming as she spoke. "Megara."

"You have no damn right to even utter my wife's name, witch!" Hercules roared.

"Yet you still do the bidding of the very gods who drove you to kill the ones you held so dear. I offer you a world without Gods who toy with you and mortals who fear you." Her words weighted heavy on both demigods. It would be so easy just to say yes and end this nonsense quest. The very people they're supposed to protect mocked and blamed them for the magic.

"Never" Abeni's golden eyes blazed like twin suns locked on the Soceresses's sliver.

"You have a point sorceress, but you forgot I chose to atone for my horrible mistakes," he said, trying to contain his anger.

The Red Sorceress sighed, shaking her head. "I would have welcomed you with open arms. Kill them all!" she ordered her followers. The bipedal wild dogs headed straight for the heart of the camp, but Abeni's sword cut down a pair while the lioness went for Hercules. Her talons would have ripped through his flesh like paper if not for his enchanted cloak that served as armor.

He swung his sword to rend the were-lioness in half, but she caught the blade with her bare hands and kicked the Son of Zeus in the gut with her strong legs. The blow knocked the wind out of him and hurled him next to the campfire. His foot kicked up the sand and smothered the flames which dispelled the Red Soceresses strange magic.

Abeni struggled to hold back the wild dogs. Her blades cutting down a few only for the remainder to bob and weave out of reach of her attacks. Lightening crackled through her fingertips as she fried a pair of them.

"We're under attack!" Shira cried as she fired an arrow. The whole camp sprang to life with weapons ready for firing at the foe. The wild dogs fell under the barrage while the swift were-lioness wove out of the way of the arrows back to her mistress' side.

"You've made a grave mistake, demigods. The people of Meroe will pay dearly for it," the Red Sorceress muttered as a sandstorm swept over where the pair once stood, leaving nothing but the bodies of the wild dog beasts.

"General Ojo, Hercules, are you alright?" Lieutenant Tabid asked as the troops lowered their bows.

"I'm fine. Thank you for the back up," General Ojo replied. Hercules was lost in thought for a moment staring out at the blood covered sands. No one had called him by his old name in years. All the world knew him as Hercules the hero. Yet, the sorceress was right that Hera had driven him mad and in the moment of madness he'd done the unthinkable.

"Like you said, you've atoned for your crimes. You've saved countless lives. You travelled here to protect not only your people, but also the world. Don't let her shake you," Abeni said bringing Hercules back to the present.

Tabid relived Hercules right away realizing that their nighttime protector needed sleep. Perhaps it would help him shake off the painful memories of the past. In the warmth of his tent, Hercules fell asleep. As soon as his head touched the pillow, he started to dream but it was unlike any dream he'd ever had. He floated above his sleeping form, watching himself toss and turn muttering incoherently in Greek. As if a string had been tied to his waist, he was pulled upwards passing through the tent's fabric like a ghost. He flew across the sky covering hundreds of miles in heart beats until he came to a burning city. Flames roared from the mud brick buildings while people fled in terror. Bouda's hunted down the survivors, pouncing on any that were too slow. But it was more than were-hyenas, a man covered in crocodile scales attacked a solider trying to protect a small group of survivors. His long jaw bit through the man's cow hide shield taking large chunks of his arms with it. With another bite he silenced his victim's pained screams.

"Soon all of Nubia will be mine." The dark-skinned woman, her face covered by a red cloak said standing the middle of the chaos. Dozens of transformed people stood at her side, some were part crocodile, other's lions, some leopards, wild dogs. It was as if she twisted the natural world and man together in a hideous union.

"It seems as we have prying eyes. I despise uninvited guests," silver eyes shone under her hood as she locked on Hercules. Somehow, she could see him. She began to mutter a spell as a sphere of flame danced in her outstretched palms, hurling it at her invisible spy. Just as the flames were about to hit Hercules, he was pulled back even further by the unseen force.

†††

Winji braved the sandstorm, the grains tearing at her skin, stinging her eyes, and clogging her throat. Her horse had died days ago, no thanks to a cobra's bite, and now she was truly alone.

Through the sand she saw a faint light in the distance, a glimmer of something. Maybe it was a village or a caravan's campsite? With renewed hope she pressed on coughing and spitting out sand with each strained breath.

"I can help you," a voice whispered. "Come to me" the sweet whispers slid into her mind easily pushing the pain and fear away. All she needed to do was get to the light. After what felt like eons, she came to the mouth of a cave, a jagged scar that ran up a giant rock. The woman scurried inside, the torches that hung on the engraved walls lit as she passed, as if this place was welcoming her. The walls were engraved with images of the gods, some she knew like Amun, and the lion headed Apedemak fighting against an entity made of pure shadow.

"They exiled me too," the voice whispered. "Pushed me out in the desert wastes, alone and forgotten."

The pain of those words went to Winji very core. She'd gone from just a humble seamstress to outcast all because of her curse. The queen had caught her talking to animals while she worked. At first, they'd deemed her crazy. But once it was shown that she could control them she was considered dangerous and dangers needed to be dealt with before they became a threat. Lost in her memories her legs carried her deeper into the cave down worn stairs and past ruined pillars eroded by nature and covered in writing. The welcoming light greeted her at the bottom. Giant statues of the Gods and Goddesses stood in a circle around a raised dais. There were unknown gods guarding the crystal, such as a woman wielding a bronze shield and spear and another woman in flowing robes holding a mirror but, they all faded into the background.

"Make them suffer. Make the ones who exiled you, who mocked you, who shunned you pay," the voice whispering in her ear grew loud enough for her to hear it outside her mind as if there was another presence in the room. In the center of the room on a dais was the blood red crystal the size of a baby's fist.

"If the Gods feared such a small thing imagine what it could do to a human? Let me awaken the true power slumbering within you," the voice commanded. The woman screamed while energy burned into her veins as if her very blood was molten lava. Winji tried to let go of the stone, but her fingers seemed possessed and tightened their grip as the pain grew worse. Forbidden magic and memories that were not her own flooded her brain so fast that her eyes rolled back into her head while the room seemed to spin around her. She dropped to her knees crying unable to bear anymore but, underneath the pain came a roaring torrent of power that engulfed her, body and soul. With one final scream that echoed in the forgotten hall Winji the Seamstress was gone and the Red Sorceress had risen.

The Son of Zeus bolted awake covered in sweat.

Tabid and Abeni raced to his tent and opened the flap. Hercules pulled his sheet around his waist suddenly shy for Abeni to see his nude form.

"You saw Meroe ablaze as well?" Abeni asked. All Hercules could do was nod. "Just ...give me a moment to get dressed."

From the way Abeni's eyes widened she just realized the nudity of the Son of Zeus and coughed awkwardly. "Yes, I'll meet you by the cook fire," she closed the tent flap. He got dressed quickly, wondering why he of all people was so awkwardly shy. He'd seen women and men naked before and shared his bed with both. But when it came to Abeni he found himself as nervous as a teen. He left the tent to find everyone eating a breakfast of dried dates, jerky and water. He joined them and ate unable to get the scent of blood and death out his nostrils. A thick trail of smoke rose from just beyond the dunes.

"Winji has sacked Meroe and her army grows as we speak. We can't let her reach Napata" Abeni said as she penned a note and attached it to the messenger hawk.

"We should head them off; we could buy the rest of your army some time. The longer we wait, the longer she has a chance to create more monstrosities," Hercules said wiping date juice from his lip with the back of his hand.

"I agree with you. Today our goal is to cover as much ground as possible. Pack up the tents we move out in five minutes!" Abeni commanded. With the help of Hercules, they were road ready in no time. They saddled up and rode towards the smoke, fear urging them forward. Every time he closed his eyes, the Son of Zeus could see the burning city, the streets filled with blood and viscera, and he could hear the moans of the dying. But the dead were the lucky ones, for he'd watched people painfully transform into bipedal animals bent on destruction. From the grim look in Abeni golden orbs, she saw it as well. Any other horses would have collapsed from the breakneck pace their riders set but these sleek and strong steeds were trained from birth for war and kept moving eager to prove themselves the swiftest of the lot. It was late in the afternoon when they finally started to show signs of fatigue. In the distance an oasis sprang up but through his sweat-drenched brow Hercules thought it was a mirage. He'd already seen a trio of busty sirens urging him to come join them, Jason calling him for another adventure and even his young sons asking to play with them. It was the burnt scent that kept him on course. It was only when Abeni pointed to the location on the map did he believe it to be real. The General steered the group to the left, off the path towards the city.

"We'll be of no help to anyone if we die of dehydration before we even reach the city."

Lush palms grew around a crystal-clear watering hole. Their water had begun to run low earlier in the day after using the last drop to keep the horses' strength from waning. The war steeds, thirsty from their long trek across the endless desert, drank deeply. Abeni kept look out, alert to any stray noise. Hercules kept his hands close to his weapons.

Tabid bent to refill his water skin, the sand shifted suddenly causing the horses to panic, a sinkhole formed sucking in anyone unlucky enough to get close to its center. Tabid was consumed instantly, sand filling his lungs before he could cry out. Another warrior fell off her horse tumbling into the sea of sand below. She pulled in vain on her horses' reins trying to loosen herself but, a giant pincer rose from the sands. Her screams of agony were silenced by a enormous Scorpion who rose from the abyss. One warrior was crushed under the monster's massive legs while another fell to pincers.

"By the Gods!" Abeni swore. "Archers, fire at will and stay out of range of its stinger!" she commanded while she drew her bow. Hercules marveled at the General's calm demeanor. Fear and panic were replaced with focus and the engrained movements of combat veterans. A volley of black arrows rained down, but none could pierce the hard carapace. With a hiss the arachnid turned its five sets of eyes to the nuisances. Not to be out done by the General, Hercules charged forward yelling at the top of his lungs.

"Over here you overgrown bug! Let's see how you stand before Athenian courage!" he yelled dodging the boat-sized pincers with his mare's speed. Another volley of arrows blotted out the sun as the Nubian archers struck again, while most struck the arachnid's natural armor Abeni's arrow hit its front cluster of eyes. Shrieking with pain the stinger the width of a boulder crashed to the ground causing the generals' troops to scatter. The trees in the oasis shriveled, turning black as the poison seeped into the ground.

Abeni knocked her arrow, preparing to fire as her electricity crackled around it. She released, it sailed across the sky striking its target. The creature shuddered, spasming from the current racing through its body, but it quickly recovered and continued the attack. The general clicked her tongue, time for a different approach. Abeni leapt from the saddle pulling her cloak's hood over her head. In an instant, she went from human to a leopardess the size of an oxen. Her strides ate up ground. She leapt and bit into the creature's middle leg, snapping it off in a gush of black blood. She danced with catlike grace and ease out of the way of the pincers.

"Hercules, take out its stinger. We'll cover you!" General Ojo cried, in a growling animal like voice. She struck again, ripping the front leg in half causing the creature to pitch forward. Her troops readied another attack. Hercules couldn't stop smiling recklessly. He leaped off his saddle and landed on the creature's right pincer. As he ran up the hard surface his shield protected him from the oncoming arrows. He stabbed deep into the scorpions' eyes; black ichor flowed from the wound. The arachnid thrashed around trying in vain to shake off the attacker, but Hercules held fast, using the beasts' natural armor as hand holds climbing up the tail. With its uneven legs it leaned on its left side struggling to support itself. Abeni ripped more legs off the beast making it pitch and sway, spraying blood everywhere. The pulsing stringer hung over head rearing back, ready to strike the archers. Using his legendary strength, Hercules pulled the bulbous stringer, his olive face turning bright red from effort. Black Ichor burst forth as the entire stringer came off. With a final cry the scorpion fell, bled out and lay unmoving. The general whispered a word that was eaten by the desert winds and became human once more. She spat out the arachnid's raven feather black blood, wiping her mouth in disgust.

A cheer rose from the remaining troops. Abeni pumped her fist in the air in triumph. Purple miasma drifted from the corpse as the arachnid began to shrink down to its normal size. To confirm it no longer posed a threat, Abeni had her horse trample it under its hooves, leaving nothing but shattered, bloody bits. Victory tasted bittersweet as Abeni noticed Tabid's waterskin stained crimson with someone's blood. Out of the ten troops they'd started with they were reduced to six.

There was a moment of silence while they remembered the fallen. Hercules hoped that their souls went to Elysium where true heroes spent eternity.

"Rest well, brothers and sisters. We will protect the kingdom. You fought with honor and courage. May your names ring out throughout history" Abeni said.

"Aera!" Shira called from the back of the troop.

"Petros" a man took up the call, his voice shaky.

"Ketti" Kinya choked out the name, tears rolled down his cheeks.

"Tabid" Abeni's voice was strong and confident. She would send the young lieutenant off with honor befitting his station, but her hands gripped the waterskin so tightly that her knuckles went ashy.

After the impromptu ceremony, Abeni mounted her steed and took out her spyglass. They were a day's ride away from Meroe.

"Do you see that?" Hercules asked squinting towards the horizon.

Abeni turned her spyglass in the direction he was looking. The ruins of the city seemed to glow with mystic energy. The miasma clung to the buildings, twisting them into thorny obstructions. The strange magic had turned the city into a supernatural jungle with black barked purple palm trees, blood red flowers the size of ox carts and grey snake- like vines. The bipedal lioness who'd fought Hercules feasted on sheep carcass.

"It grows worse by the day" Hercules muttered. Abeni looked at her worn, disheartened troops. She knew they needed rest and time to mourn the loss of their comrades in arms. But, at the rate the spell was taking hold, it could reach the capital in a matter of days.

"Refill your waterskins and let the horses drink their fill. Then we ride through the night for the city or what was once Meroe."

Worn, scared faces looked back at her and gave a solemn nod.

†††

Abeni rode in the vanguard with Hercules by her side while the six remaining troops pulled up the rear.

"You did what you could," Hercules said breaking the companionable silence.

"If I had trained them better or drilled them harder…" she swore to herself in a low voice that only the demigod could hear.

"It was a surprise attack by a creature no one even knew existed. You trained them well and you have six lives to prove it."

"Son of Zeus, when you are not punching things there may be more than rocks in that head of yours," Abeni said.

Hercules comically tapped his fist against his skull which made Abeni laugh. Riding all night into place of danger and certain death, Abeni's charming belly laugh eased the bow string taunt air of tension. If she was going to die tomorrow, at least let tonight be worth remembering. Watered and fed, the war horses moved with ease across the dunes, eating up ground with their frantic pace. They ate dinner in their saddles, making short work of goat jerky and savoring cool, fresh water. Some mutters prayers to Amesemi, the lion headed goddess of war. Abeni whispered her father's name hoping he could hear her. Even Hercules called on Athena for wisdom and Aeres for courage in battle adding a cry to Zeus hoping against hope to be heard.

The coppery scent of blood was so strong that they could taste it in the very air. Instead of arriving at the city walls, they came to a verdant jungle full of plants that seemed to belong not on earth but in Persephone's Garden. The black bark trees grew in clusters too close for the horses to get through, so the group dismounted.

"Stay close and keep your eyes peeled. It's more than just monsters that await us within," General Ojo said.

Barely any moonlight reached through the thick canopy; however Abeni maneuvered in the low light which must have been one of her gifts as a demi-god. Hercules followed; the strange cries of unfamiliar creatures and eerie birdsong which put him on edge. The cries were so warped and distorted into strange facsimiles by the dark magic that each sound made his skin crawl. Even with one the soldiers carrying a lit torch, those without Abeni's sight could see only a few feet in front of them. Where the son of Zeus was hesitant, the daughter of Shango was confident. Her strides left almost no tracks on the wet earth as she moved gingerly through the jungle. It was hard to believe that this place had literally sprung up overnight.

A playful giggle echoed all around them. "I see you" said a young woman's sing song voice. In the dim light a shadow slithered behind them. Before Abeni could cry out, a vine wrapped around Shira's neck, the archer in the rear. Shira screamed only to be jerked upwards by an invisible force. The motion was so sudden and forceful that her neck snapped instantly.

"Where are you, damn witch?!" the torch bearer cried. "FACE ME!" he yelled into the shadow jungle. The only reply was harsh, biting laughter.

"Kinya, silence," Abeni whispered.

"She killed my sister!" he yelled loudly. Hercules clamped a hand over the panicked soldier's mouth.

"Listen here and listen well. Shira wouldn't want you to die a fool's death. If you want to live to avenge her, shut your mouth or I'll gag you. I won't let you put the rest of my troop in needless danger," Abeni snapped softly. Kinya's pained expression was made sharper by the torchlight. There was clearly more that he wanted to say but the look in Abeni's eyes left no room for argument.

"STAY CLOSE AND KEEP YOUR EYES PEELED."

Hercules removed his hand and Kinya followed General Abeni deeper in the waking nightmare.

A slick, wet substance dripped down from the branches above. Kinya wiped his face only to see his hand covered in crimson. In the torchlight a pair of reflective yellow eyes shone back. The archer behind him loosed an arrow. In an instant the were-lioness leapt from her perch and snapped it in half with her fangs. Kinya waved the torch frantically, hoping the fire would keep the big cat at bay, but human intelligence reflected in her eyes. She blew out the torch and plunged them into darkness.

A gargled scream tore from Kinya's throat in a darkness so thick that even Abeni had trouble finding her way. Bathing her body in lightening she turned into a human torch only to find Kinya's neck torn out and the other archer laying in a pool of blood.

"I granted Kinya's wish. Who else wants to join him?" The sorceress said with a chuckle. The three remaining troops were driven to the point of panic. Hercules couldn't blame them in this unnatural place death lurked around every corner.

"Stay close to me" General Abeni ordered using her hand to light Hercules' spare torch. The three archers had their arrows knocked and ready, aiming at the slightest sound. After all the were-lioness was still roaming about the bush with a taste for blood. They traveled in silence; not daring to look down as their sandals crunched on what they fervently hoped was fallen tree branches that snapped under foot. Suddenly frantic crying could be heard, aching sobs that reminded Hercules of his own children from what felt like a lifetime ago. The sound could have been that of a group of children who managed to survive the chaos and hid somewhere.

"It could be a trap" Abeni said reaching for her blades. "Or it could be the only group of survivors" Hercules's counter point was accentuated by high-pitched screams of a child followed by the were-lioness's roar. Hercules sprinted ahead; Abeni followed swearing in every language she knew.

"Cover him!" she ordered. After what felt like forever, they came to a clearing. A pair of young girls were perched in black trees while the were-lioness stalking circled the base, licking her bloodstained lips. A third girl lay unmoving at the bottom. From her body's angle, she must have panicked and fell out the tree.

"Get away from them!" Hercules called, banging his sword against his shield to get the creatures attention. She turned and stood on her hindlegs, towering over him at seven feet.

"I have heard that the blood of a demigod tastes like nectar. I can't wait to find out if that's true." Her guttural voice scratched his ear drums. A trio of arrows came from behind him as General Ojo and her archers caught up. Her razor-sharp talons cut them out of the air in moments as turned her full attention the Greek demigod. He blocked, her nails raking against the stylized medusa head on his bronze shield. She tried to kick his legs out from under him; instead he shifted and threw his weight behind his shield knocking her down. Hercules pushed with all his might until he heard the snap of broken ribs. The were-lioness gasped; her rib punctured lungs were suffocating her instantly.

Abeni climbed up the tree, while the were-lioness was occupied, and retrieved the girls who now clung to her back. As soon as Abeni's feet touched the ground she screamed as a knife sunk into her shoulder. The tallest child jumped off her back.

"You really are far too soft hearted for a warrior, General." The girl transformed into the red robed woman from the demigods shared dream. Winji was a natural beauty with ebony skin dotted with small scarification bumps that created an oval pattern around her silver eyes and continued to her checks and forehead, however, crystal spikes jutted from her shoulders and up her arms marring her beauty. Over the years, the dark magical item had fused to her very soul. Her short black hair was done in fine braids. Her cloak covered her clothing, but her silver eyes gleamed. Her full lips parted into a cruel smile.

The little girl who looked no older than six, clung to Abeni who staggered to her feet shielding her with her body. A volley of arrows raced towards the Red Sorceress who danced between them. A were-serpent with cobra hood flared pounced from the brushes beside the archers. Venomous fangs bit into their bare flesh before they could retaliate. They collapsed spasming in agony eventually lying still. Hercules caught the serpents' neck as it tried to bite his shoulder, he snapped its neck hoping the soldiers' souls could rest knowing that their deaths had been avenged.

"Why do you want to play protector for fickle, old humanity?" Winji asked. "You come from afar to aid them and yet they blame you for the cause."

The words of the crowd in Napata drifted back into his mind. They had been more than willing to turn on both Abeni and him if that one stranger hadn't stuck up for them.

"The moment I showed powers, they ran me out of the kingdom. I, Winji, the same girl they came to sew their clothes and hem their dresses. Even Queen Ashri had me design clothes for her son." For a moment she seemed to have forgotten that they were there, lost in some past grievance. Her silver eyes glowed red, the same color as the gem, the size of a baby's fist, which was embedded into her neck as having long since fused with her flesh.

"Queen Ashri? That was Queen Unatti's great ancestor! So, you take your anger out on innocent people centuries later?" Abeni questioned with swords in hand.

"Innocent? They all deserve to suffer," she cried bitterly as creatures swarmed from the forest, the crystal glowing yet again as they attacked.

They were the only people left alive. Winji's monsters had made short work of the brave archers that had followed them into this hellish place. Lightening electrified Abeni's twin blades causing them to shine in the dim light. Hercules tightened his grip on his enchanted bronze sword, the blade already slick with blood soon to be quenched in more.

The only ones that stood between the innocent souls in Napata were a pair of weary demigods. The short haired sorceress laughed as if her senseless bloodshed was nothing more than a game.

"If we each take one hundred, we should make it out alive," Abeni said concealing her heart-pounding fear. If Winji's beasts broke through, they would spread a reign of terror and death, growing their numbers with each city and town they came across. By the time they reached Rhakotis, they could easily cross the Aegean and spread their terror throughout known world. Abeni strength and determination to defeat the witch was the knowledge that the only untransformed survivor of the once thriving city cowered behind her. Hercules drew a line in the sand behind him.

"I swear by Zeus and all the Olympians that none shall cross this line!" he yelled, his voice hoarse. "I'll take the hundred on the right." After spending a few days with him, Abeni could tell his bravado was as false as her own. Like her, Hercules was willing to fight to the death he too realized what was at stake.

"Hide" Hercules whispered to the child as he unpinned his cloak and wrapped her in it. She ran past the pair and hid behind a tree. Now she'd be protected by the tree and the cloak from any stray spells or savage attacks from beasts that broke through their ranks. Without his cloak, Hercules was left vulnerable. For a moment he thought of his own sons cowering in terror. He would let no child suffer ever again.

Winji smiled, white teeth flashing against dark skin. "You're a true Greek, Son of Zeus. A lover of tragedies to the bitter end."

The army charged, their war cries a cacophony of ear-splitting, disjointed, and strange noises. Abeni's blades tore into the Crocodile whose wide jaws were aimed at her head. If being impaled on blades didn't kill him, the electricity that coursed through his veins would leave him smoked and charred like a croc on the spit. The general withdrew her weapons dodging a Bouda with the speed of the wind. She dashed into the menagerie cutting down anyone in her path, her speed making her a harder target. She leapt into the air, grabbing on a tree branch, and nodded at the son of Zeus. Hercules' shield slammed into the ground, cracking the earth open, the ground beneath a dozen creatures crumbled violently, sending them falling into the pitch-black void. Winji jumped backwards missing the fall by inches. Abeni dove from above, beheading a pair of cobra-headed monsters who were positioned to spit venom at Hercules.

Seeing her army in disarray, the sorceress began tossing fireballs. Abeni dodged and rolled, the ends of her braids were singed by the flames that tore a hole in the tree behind her. She froze as the trireme sized trunk fell towards her. Hercules gripped the burning trunk as Abeni went flat on the ground. He swung the sixteen-foot tree like a club. Bones crunched; beasts yelped in pain as the giant club slammed into them. Abeni hopped to her feet, focusing her lightening between her palms, the static making her hair stand on end. Strands of electricity arced, hitting the remaining creatures, turning them into fried bodies.

"Worn out already?" Winji mocked as Abeni wheezed and Hercules dropped his club, tiredness sinking into his bones. As the dust settled, more creatures came out of the shadowy tree line, ready and waiting to strike. The sorceress had hidden the true strength of her forces and now they would be overrun.

Abeni looked back at the girl in hiding who'd curled up, hugging her knees, and shutting her eyes tight, wrapped in the cloak like a blanket. Even if she could protect just one person from this mad Sorceress, she would die happy.

"She reminds me of my kids" Hercules said panting. "I've lost my family I won't let anyone take another innocent life."

"Hercules, I can hold them off. Smash the crystal. It's the source of her power," Abeni whispered, remembering the shared dream, as she started to float above the tree line whipping the trees with hurricane force winds. She raised her hands above her head and lightning bolts struck whichever unlucky beast she pointed at. Creatures that had been ready to kill one minute were reduced to ashes the next. The more she discharged her power the lower she began to float and wobble in the air. Sweat drenched her brow as she struggling to keep her the raw force of lightning under control. It felt like trying to hold back a stampede of wild horses with nothing but a frayed rope.

"Stop her! She'll ruin everything!" Winji cried calling more beasts to her aid. Hercules wasn't known for being stealthy, a 6'9 olive-skinned Athenian man normally couldn't sneak up on a blind man but in the chaos of battle and over the roaring cracks of lightening and blinding flashes of light, he was practically invisible since the Red Sorceress was solely focused subduing the Daughter of Shango. Wordlessly, Hercules charged just as the lightening flashed one final time and Abeni fell to earth creating a small crater in her wake. His sword not only ran the sorceress through but also pierced the crystal.

The Red Sorceress blew away like dust in the wind as the ruby crystal shattered. A crisp, joyous laugh tore through the air. "See, that's what you get for calling the power stories 'trivial'. Now that was a fine tale!"

A shirtless youth walked out of the jungle in a crimson jacket. His dreads were short and decorated with cowrie shells. Abeni staggered to her feet, dazed. Save for being covered in dirt and the blood of her foes she was unharmed. She scrambled out of the crater. Both demigods drew their weapons ready to strike, although Abeni leaned against Hercules for a few moments to stop her head from spinning like a whirlwind. The youth threw up his hands.

"It was dicey in the middle there; I couldn't see where the strands were going but you two proved quite capable."

"Who are you?!" Abeni snapped, steadying herself.

"Anansi, the God of Stories," he gave a theatrical bow.

"Did you cook up this threat for your own amusement?" Hercules added.

Anansi looked shocked and appalled. "I saw a thread of danger that if not handled would spread across the world, so I simply crossed a few threads and entered your dreams to give you a little push in the right direction." he smiled turning into Pallas Athena and then into Shango before turning back to the wry youth once more.

"What about my troops? Did they need to die?" Abeni trembled with rage in memory of the warriors she'd personally trained. They'd become more than troops: they'd been her friends.

"You two really did save lives, stopped a very real threat and created unity between your peoples. I just interfered where it was necessary. This was the strand of the tale that ended with the least deaths. If you had seen what had happened in others you would have agreed with me too. I will make sure that they are never forgotten in this tale." A storm cloud rolled in, lightning and thunder crashing.

"And... I've got to run. Looks like Shango and the others are back from their little stay in the underworld." Anansi hastily replied suddenly standing in between the demigods, placing his hands on both their shoulders. With a swift pull, he removed the dagger from Abeni's right shoulder blade. He placed his hand over the wound, and it healed leaving a pink scar. A soothing warmth spread through both demigods leaving them both feeling refreshed and well rested.

"Gotta add to the legend" he said with a wink.

"Wait, you imprisoned both pantheons in the UNDERWORLD?!" Hercules yelled.

"Only for the duration of your quest to make sure they didn't fall prey to the Red Sorceress's power. She'd been craving their abilities for centuries. She overlooked me since she thought stories have no power." A tangled web shot out from his palm entangling shards of the ruby that had scattered in the wake of Winji's destruction. "Both pantheons will be sure to scatter this to the far corners of space. After all, you saw what one vengeful ghost could do with it in only a matter of days. If a magical mortal or demigod had gotten their hands on it, things could have been a lot worse. Rest, enjoy your victory and know you have saved the world. There may be other trials ahead for both of you."

With that the youth left, humming a tune to himself. The pair of demigods gave a sigh of relief as the forest died around them. Without Winji's crystal to sustain them they simply ceased to be, leaving the ruins of Meroe in their place. Scorched and crumbling mud brick homes, shattered stalls and blood splattered streets were the grim reminders of the carnage. The bestial people turned from monsters back into confused citizens.

"Duwana!" one of the newly freed women cried. The girl who had hidden behind the tree ran towards her mother with tears in her eyes, tossing aside the lion pelt cloak which Hercules caught.

"Mama! Mama! The nice people saved me!" she said in between being smothered with hugs and kisses.

"Anansi is right about one thing, this is cause for celebration, both to honor the dead and to instill hope in the living and I think my people do parties best" Abeni said with a smile.

"You haven't dined in my hall, Abeni. We party from sun to sun." Hercules replied jokily as hundreds of horses mounted with soldiers came over the horizon with the Queen herself leading the charge. Dressed in full armor with a bejeweled sword in one hand and the other on the reins of a tall war horse, she looked ready to slay an army single handedly.

"You two took on a whole army and saved my citizens?" the queen said in shock staring at the bloody ruined city. Her soldiers murmured in shock at the two blood covered demigods who hadn't just held off an army but had defeated one.

"It's quite a tale to tell, your Highness," Hercules said. He and Abeni traded off parts of the tale making sure to praise the troops as much as possible. Without realizing it, the pair transfixed both the army and the newly freed citizens who were waiting with bated breath to see how each new challenge in the tale was overcome.

Once the tale was done, mourning the dead came before celebrating the living. The Queen ordered a two-week mourning period to honor the fallen troops and innocents lost. The palace hired the best stone masons in the capital to build their graves. The entire troop that had fought alongside the General and Hercules was post humorously promoted to the rank of General to honor their courage and sacrifice. Their families were paid full pensions.

Shira and Kinya's parents tearfully embraced the demigods.

"Thank you General, for trying your best to protect my children." Their mother managed to blurt out in between sobs.

"It was an honor to serve with them," Abeni said.

"Even though I was a foreigner, they treated me with kindness and friendship. I will never forget them" Hercules added. Since Tabid was an orphan, Abeni paid for his funeral rites personally as if he were her own brother.

The troops were mummified and interred in small pyramids which normally housed the bodies of the wealthy or the nobility. Rebuilding Meroe came next. While the damage was extensive, buildings could be rebuilt but the dead could not. Surprisingly, since most of the people in the city had been turned into were creatures, once the spell was lifted, they reverted to their normal selves with hazy, dream-like memories of what happened. Thus, there were many helping hands in the rebuilding. With Hercules's strength and Abeni overseeing the project personally what could have taken months instead took weeks. An Obelisk was erected in the city center to remember the fallen and the story of the brave heroes and heroines who stood against the Red Sorceress.

The night the last building was completed wine flowed as freely as well water. Musicians played while people danced and sang. After so much death celebrating simply being alive brought people joy. Storytellers kept kids enthralled with tales while vendors sold anything one could ask for as the stars twinkled above them.

The demigods wandered the streets taking in the joyous sights and delicious smells. The laughter of children was a welcome change to hearing the groans of the dying and the sobs of mourning. Everyone they passed hailed them as heroes, some asking them to join in a dance, or hear a tale or have a meal on the house. They respectfully declined while walking to the city's outskirts.

"You know, Son of Zeus, I've heard rumors that a flock of Griffons have made a large nest off the coast of Greece and have been attacking ships and terrorizing the port towns. Queen Unatti has given me two months leave in honor of my service," Abeni said sipping Grecian wine with a sly smile.

"Well, I do know a trustworthy captain who could help us track them down. I would love to show you the wonders of Greece like you have shown me the charm and splendor of Nubia." Hercules replied sensing a new adventure on the horizon. Perhaps the God of Stories had more tales in store for them.

THE END

On the Creation of Hercules and the Wrath of the Red Sorceress

I was raised on myths and legends. Having parents from the Caribbean country of Jamaica, my mother kept the oral tradition of Anansi stories alive and well in my youth. As a child I even penned my own tales about the trickster spider and his cunning plans. Anansi is a unique mythological figure that bridges the cultural gap between North Africa, the Caribbean and even some parts of South America. His legends traveled with the slave trade and became tales of hope and power to a people so far away from home. He took on unique characteristics in each place, with the African Anansi having not just a wife but multiple children while the Caribbean counterpart is more known for tricks being against slave masters and Bere Rabbit. When I started this story, I knew he would have to play a role, but this is a tale about Hercules, Greece's most famous hero. How do you work in a North African God into a Greek story? Simple, connect it to North Africa. Thus, the striking opening scene was born. As for Greek mythology, I fell in love with it thanks to spending my first bit of allowance money on an illustrated edition of Greek myths. Ever since then I was hooked.

Now, while Greek myth is rather commonplace, since it's taught in schools alongside the history of ancient Greece, the varied and wonderful myths of Africa are not. When it came to learning about African myths that was a more recent passion of mine spurred by a very personal quest to define what it means to be a black woman I was inspired by towering historical figures like Queen Amina of Zazzu in Nigeria who was a military genius, building defensive walls around the cities, she captured which still stand to this day; Queen Nzinga of Ndongo and Matamba whose military prowess, cunning strategists outwitted the British. Female scholars, griots, warriors, and leaders dot the entire continent of Africa. Abeni was born from being engrossed in the fascinating lives and trials of these women from across the continent and wanting to create character that embodied that spirit. Having grown a special love for the culture of the Yoruba tribe of Nigeria, thanks to the amazing works of Nnedi Okorafor, I decided to have Abeni's divine parentage come from the

72

Orisha Pantheon. Although lesser known, this collection of deities is just as complex as and rich as the Greek Pantheon. Shango was an easy choice for her father since he plays a huge role in the Pantheon. Once a mortal king of the same name, he hung himself after accidently causing his wife and kids to be struck by lightning. After climbing a golden chain to heavens, he became the Shango, God of lightening, fire with his major symbol being a double headed axe known as an *Oshe*. Even Abeni's hair is important. Dada hair is another cultural reference found in both Igbo and Yoruba cultures. Children who are born with hair that forms natural dreads are called Dada and seen as magical. Ile-Ife, in modern Nigeria is referred to as just Ife is a city sacred to the Yoruba people as it was supposedly founded the Supreme God called Olorun and the father of all the Orisha's called Obatala.

The way we are taught history in the halls of academia is piecemeal without seeing how each culture connects to the larger picture. Which is why I chose Nubia as my central setting. Despite playing a large role in the history of Ancient Egypt and being a hub for trade between sub–Saharan Africa and the Mediterranean, Nubia is forgotten to time. Overshadowed by its upper Nile cousin, I wanted to give it a moment in the spotlight. I also wanted to show how truly interconnected the ancient world was by having these two demigods from vastly different pantheons be forced to work together in a land that is not home for either party. Even the Nubian pantheon itself is forgotten. The great starting point for research that is the internet has scattered tidbits naming a few deities but no cohesive mythology to speak of mainly mentioning how their gods simply got amalgamated into the Egyptian pantheon due to the similarities. If it wasn't for me owning a copy of an amazing black indie comic called Black Sands The Seven Kingdoms, I would have been left in the dark.

On the use of ritual scarification, many tribes in northern Africa used the practice as everything from beauty marks, part of a coming-of-age ritual or to distinguish tribe members from one another. In Yoruba culture people with said markings traditionally make the bearer be seen as trustworthy.

All this research and love culminated into the birth of my pulp take on Hercules. The pulp genre is so vast and wide that it's like a writers playground to explore ideas and concepts to no end which is what brought me to the genre.

✝✝✝

ELIZABETH FREEMAN - has always loved books and writing for as long as she can remember. She writes the kind of heroes and heroines her younger self would have loved to see. A voracious reader, she is captivated by fantasy novels as well as world mythology and folklore. Drawing inspiration from everyone from Homer to Naoko Takeuchi and dozens of creators in between inspires her to create her exciting worlds and characters. When she's not writing, she's addicted to anime, manga and comics in general and loves Chinese and Korean dramas on Netflix. After earning a bachelor's degree in English Writing from LIU Post, she went on to receive an M.F.A in Creative Writing from Hofstra University.

JOHN HENRY VS THE VAMPIRES

BY ERIC ESQUIVEL

When ol' John Henry swung his sledgehammer into solid rock, it fell harder than lightning. Made a sound louder than thunder. And left a crater in its wake that was wide enough to fit all the sins of man.

So mighty were his blows, some folks alleged that the wooden handle of John's hammer's was crafted from a fragment of The True Cross, blessed by Our Lord and anointed by the blood of his only son—that's the only way it could be strong enough to withstand John's superhuman grip without shattering into a thousand tiny splinters.

John Henry was the kind of man who left a trail of tall tales in his wake. The man was seven feet tall if he was an inch, black as a shadow, and easily three hundred pound of pure muscle. And the way he wielded that hammer gave folks the impression that he was born to. There was speculation that John's father was the Norse God "Thor" and his mother was the very Night herself.

Of course, that was all hogwash. There was a simple reason why John was as strong, tough, and smart as he was. And that's because he was a former slave. In order to endure that kind of living Hell, a man had to be damn near mythological.

And that's exactly the thought that O'Brien, his fellow "steel drivin' man", had in his head as he watched John absolutely obliterate a massive boulder without so much as furrowing his brow.

O'Brien took one last drag off of his cigarette, then quipped in a thick Irish brogue, "Slow down a mite, will yah big guy? You're fixin' ta make your fellow hammer-man look lazy in comparison."

When The Apache Railway Company set about carving tunnels through mountains for their railroads to pass through, they generally employed teams of four men (a "shaker" to hold a steel spike ready, a couple of "hammer-men" to take turns pounding that spike as far as they could into solid stone, and a "blaster" to fill those holes with enough dynamite to wake the Devil) and gave them six months in which to do it. When John Henry was on the job, it only took three. And that's because, when the other men on his team were taking their lunch, smoke, and water breaks, John pressed on—taking his hammer to the mountain itself and doing just as much damage by himself as he did with the help of his three companions.

Cruz, the team's shaker, looked up from his dry bologna sandwich and quirked an eyebrow at O'Brien.

"You don't need John's help in that department, amigo," he said. "I've never seen one man take so many smoke breaks. You must've been born with a third lung in there."

O'Brien pressed the back of his right hand against his forehead and did his best impression of a wilting flower.

"Señor, I am goin' ta go ahead and choose to forgive your ignorance, because I know you choose ta read those trashy, Mexican-language 'Tijuana Bibles' on your off-time instead of listenin' ta the radio like a good, honest American—but these particular cigarillos are Morleys. As in 'nine outta ten doctors recommend Morley's' cigarettes'."

Their team's resident blaster,—a short and soft-spoken Chinese fellow named "Zhao"—chimed in.

"Good, honest American?" Zhao asked. "I have caught you more cheating at cards more times than I can count...and you somehow still owe me two whole dollars."

Cruz walked over to John Henry and clapped a hand on his massive shoulder. "Don't you pay these slackers any bit of mind, John" he said. "I find your work ethic inspiring."

"Yeah, well, just make sure the two o' you don't wind up like Big Al", O'Brien said.

He was referencing a co-worker of theirs who—according to their foreman, Mr. Davis, had complained about being exhausted by the workload, and abandoned his post under cover of night, without so much as a polite "see you boys later" to the men he'd worked alongside, broken bread with, and bunked next to for the last quarter of a year.

An uneasy quiet fell over the worksite.

John Henry was a man of few words. And when it came to his past, he never said anything at all. So the other guys had no reason to know this. But, back before the war, John and the man folks referred to now as "Big Al" lived and worked on the same plantation. Big Al (who went by "Alfred" back in those days), was a few years John's senior. When John Henry arrived on the plantation, Alfred took John under his wing and gave him the lay of the land. Back in those days, John Henry wasn't the kind of person who took kindly to advice from strangers, elders or not. But something about the big, "X" shaped scar over Alfred's face told John Henry that "Big Al" had seen his fair share of horror on the plantation, and he was just trying to make sure that John Henry didn't see the same. Alfred was the one who instilled in John Henry the idea that a man in their situation was only as valuable as he was a hard worker. The other men all thought that John and Al were crazy for breaking their backs the way they did when they were in the field... but it wound up being a surefire way to incur their masters' favor, and avoid being treated like those poor, unfortunate souls who they considered to be dispensable.

Today, it was easily ninety five degrees outside in the Arizona heat...but just thinking back to that time sent an ice-cold chill up John Henry's spine.

Point being: John had seen Big Al work way harder, under way worse conditions than the one they presently found themselves in...and the man never once complained about "exhaustion" back then.

"...You've heard the rumors?" Zhao asked.

John Henry grimaced. He had.

Cruz nodded his head.

O'Brien's eyes widened. "How come nobody ever tells me anythin'?" he whined.

"Because you never stop talking long enough for anyone else to get a word in?" offered John Henry.

"Must be that third lung we were talking about," said Cruz.

O'Brien mimicked being shot in the heart by an arrow. "You wound me, sir".

"Well..." Zhao went on. "You know how...unsentimental...the foreman is about his workers. Some people say that they would not be surprised if Big Al died of a heart attack, and Davis just unceremoniously rolled his body into the gulch."

"The version of the rumor I heard, it wasn't a heart attack," John Henry said. "An infection. From an animal. Some rabid bat swooped down and bit him on the neck while the old man was asleep. Foreman couldn't bear to part with the coin required for a visit from the doctor, so he told him to 'walk it off'."

"Well...it sure sounds like he ain't walkin' anymore..." O'Brien said. It was a joke, but there was a fiery anger in his eyes.

Zhao said something in his native tongue, and then spit in the sand. Neither John, nor Cruz, nor O'Brien spoke Mandarin...but all three of them understood exactly what he meant.

After a moment, Cruz said aloud what everyone else was thinking: "Do they have any proof? Has anyone actually seen a body?"

Zhao pointed to the clouds. Way, way off in the distance, three vultures patiently circle the train.

"No. But those buzzards have clearly seen something that piques their interest."

"Not necessarily," Cruz corrected. "You might not know this, not having grown up in the desert—but you don't always see vultures because there's a dead body nearby. Sometimes they're just following a predator—like a mountain lion, or a coyote—and waiting for one to drop."

"So you're tellin' me our options are either: there's a conspiracy ta cover-up our friend's untimely death. Or there's a giant tangle of fangs and claws out there, stalking our site?" O'Brien asked.

"That's pretty much the gist of it, yeah," Cruz shrugged.

The high-pitched sound of a steam whistle echoed off the canyon walls, alerting the workers to the end of their workday shift.

O'Brien dropped his cigarette and ground its glowing red embers into the sand with the toe of his leather work boot.

"Right. Well. Lovely workin' with you as always, gentlemen." O'Brien bowed. "If anyone needs me, I'll be gettin' absolutely blackout-drunk in me tent."

Zhao stood on his tippy-toes and stretched as far as his arms could reach. His right elbow made an odd popping sound, like the opening of a glass bottle of Coke.

"I think I'll join you," Zhao yawned.

Cruz heaved his sledge onto his shoulder, and let his tin lunch box dangle off the head of the hammer. From a distance, he looked like a cartoon hobo with a bindle.

"What kind of trouble are you getting up to tonight, John?" Cruz asked.

"Got me a date with a beautiful redhead," John smiled.

Cruz laughed. "Well, tell that Miss Clementine I send my love."

"Will do, sir. Will do" John Henry replied.

John Henry had a standing date with Miss Clementine every night at seven o'clock. And she was never, ever late. Which was considerably more impressive when one considered that she didn't own a watch. Or even have an arm on which to wear one.

Miss Clementine (or, "Clemmy", if you were a member of her inner circle) was a cat. One of the more talkative species, a bright orange body and dark patches of brown fur across her back, paws, and face.

Just like everyone else who orbited The Kokopelli Express, Miss Clementine had a job to do. It was her lot in life to patrol both the train and the surrounding campsite (where the workers set up their tents at night), and keep them free from vermin. Miss Clementine was a tough old broad—she lost her left eye to a scorpion's sting, and had a chunk of her right ear taken out by a desert rat who vehemently disagreed with her decision to eat him. But, every night at seven sharp, she made her way over to John Henry's campsite and curled up in his lap like a newborn kitten as he read to her, by the light of his kerosene lamp, from whatever dime store "penny dreadful" he was currently working his way through.

Reading was a new pleasure for John Henry. Having learned to read relatively recently, the literature available to him, at his reading level, tended to be simple morality tales featuring Good Vs. Evil. Masked mystery men versus dastardly villains. Brave astronauts versus ray-gun-wielding space tyrants. Knights in gleaming armor versus fire-spewing dragons. And John wouldn't have it any other way. The real world was so often a depressing place; full of ethical ambiguity...It was nice to spend an hour or so every night reading about worlds wherein good old-fashioned heroism was still possible.

Tonight, John Henry was reading to Clementine from a short story included between the covers of Super Thrilling Action Magazine, entitled "Jax Meteor: Martian Iron." It was about a nomadic, green-skinned, four-armed gunslinger who traversed the sands of Mars on the back of a giant ant—stumbling into adventure as he searched for his missing fiancé.

"Jax's insectoid steed bucked so hard, he nearly threw the man off his saddle," John Henry read aloud. He spoke slowly and deliberately as he sounded out each word. And he slid his calloused right pointer-finger across the page, underlining each word so that he didn't lose his place.

Clementine rewarded John's efforts by nuzzling up against his stomach and purring as loudly as she was physically capable of.

John smiled. He patted her on the head, as a way to thank her for letting him practice his reading on her. Someday—after he had accumulated enough of a "nest egg" from working his hands to the bone on the railroad—John Henry hoped to settle down with a wife and children. A wife and children who he could read to at night, as they drifted off to sleep in his arms. Until then, furry little Clementine would do just fine.

"Jax yanked on the bug's reigns and shouted in a strong, steady voice: 'calm your mandibles, you skittering—'"

John's reading was interrupted by the sound of a twig snapping a couple yards behind him. John—hyper-vigilant after all the talk of mountain lions and coyotes from earlier—leaped to his feet and grabbed his work-hammer.

Clementine fell from his lap and landed on all-fours. She arched her back, barred her claws, and hissed for all she was worth.

Both Clementine and John Henry held their ground, waiting for their heretofore unseen threat to emerge from the shadows and make its play for their respective jugulars.

"Are you out of your cotton-pickin' mind, boy?" Mr. Davis shouted. Moonlight glinted off the barrel of the sawed-off shotgun the foreman held in his hands. "Put that hammer down!"

The foreman talked tough. But John Henry noticed that his hands were trembling.

John Henry dropped his hammer. The impact send shockwaves through earth so powerful, they just about knocked Mr. Davis on his wide rear-end.

Clementine, upon seeing John's posture change, stopped hissing and retracted her claws.

Mr. Davis lowered his gun.

"I'm sorry, sir" John said. "I didn't realize you were...well, you."

John furrowed his brow as he thought for a moment. "If you don't mind me asking: why are you walking around the campsite after-hours, sir? If I had my own train car to sleep in at night, I—"

"Well, you don't. Do you?" Mr. Davis asked.

John looked down at the ground.

"No, sir. No I do not."

Mr. Davis grunted. John understood what it meant. And he hated him for it. But John's hatred was wasn't visible, or loud. It was a quiet, smoldering feeling. And a familiar one. One he desperately wished he could evacuate from his heart, but doubted he'd ever have the spiritual strength to.

"Truth be told, I was out here looking for bandidos."

"'Bandidos', sir?"

"Bandits, son. 'Bandidos' it's Mexican for 'bandits'. Some of the boys have reported seeing some ne'er-do-well in a black poncho, wandering around the campsite. Probably scrounging for food and scrap to steal. You know how those types are always looking for a handout."

John Henry fought the urge to roll his eyes. Cruz was Mexican-American ("one of those types"), and John Henry struggled to think of anyone he'd ever met who was more honest, or hardworking.

"And you thought he was bunking with me, sir?" John Henry asked.

Mr. Davis spit a wad of brown-green chewing tobacco into the sand.

"Heard you flapping your jaw out here. Seemed only logical to assume you mighta had company."

John Henry gestured towards the copy of Super Thrilling Action Magazine, which sat by his lantern.

"I was reading."

"Out loud?" Mr. Davis asked. "To yourself?"

John nodded towards Clementine. "To Clemmy."

Mr. Davis walked over to the magazine and picked it up.

"Our company mascot's a Science Fiction fan, is she?"

John's cheeks grew warm.

"I don't think she's much particular about genres, sir. She just likes the attention. And I like the stories. So it's a good fit."

Mr. Davis examined the magazine's cover. This particular edition of Super Thrilling Action featured a painted cover by Earle K. Bergey, depicting Jax Meteor with a ray-gun in each of his four, three-fingered hands.

"Huh," Mr. Davis said, bemused. "I didn't know they had nigrahs in space."

John Henry looked at the stars. "I don't imagine, in real life, they've got much of anyone up there. White, or Black."

John pointed at the cover of the magazine.

"But I do have to point out that the character you're referring to is of the green-skinned persuasion. So your comment about him being a 'nigger' might not be all-the-way accurate."

Mr. Davis screwed his face up, like he was confused.

"You're saying just because a man's green, he can't be a nigrah? I look around this site everyday, and you know what I see? Chinese nigrahs. Mexican nigrahs. Hell, we even got Irish nigrahs. 'Nigrah' just means 'non-white'. And that ugly green bastard sure ain't white, is he?"

John Henry didn't know whether to cry, or to laugh. The foreman's willful ignorance was so astounding...it was almost impressive. Here John was, teaching himself how to read and write after a lifetime of being forcefully denied his right to an education...while Mr. Davis was doing the opposite; equally as committed to his own stupidity as John Henry was to his self-improvement. What a world. Every bit as alien and insane as that of Jax Meteor, and his dime story adventures.

"He sure isn't, Mr. Davis. I understand your point. Thank you for being patient and teaching it to me, sir."

Mr. Davis raised an eyebrow at John. John Henry often spoke to him in a way that seemed respectful—all the words were right, on paper—but still seemed sarcastic. When he was a child, Mr. Davis and his peers used to torment and throw rocks at a mentally-slow peer who they nicknamed "The Professor". When John Henry called Mr. Davis "sir" it reminded Mr. Davis of the exact same faux-respectful tone that Mr. Davis and his peers used to refer to that unfortunate boy. And Mr. Davis hated him for that.

"You know what—?" Mr. Davis started to ask. But he never finished his thought. Because, just as he opened his mouth, he was interrupted by a blood-curdling scream, from across the campsite.

†††

By the time John Henry and Mr. Davis arrived at the source of the scream, the sounds of fear had been replaced by a wave of rowdy laughter.

"Oi! It ain't funny!" O'Brien—who was as red in the face as John had ever seen him—shouted at the assembled crowd.

John shouldered his way through the throng of guffawing onlookers, so he could sidle-up next to Cruz and Zhao.

"Anyone wanna fill me in?" John asked.

Cruz was still chuckling as he wiped tears from the corners of his eyes. "It seems your co-hammer-man saw a ghost..."

John Henry cocked his head to the side. "That's weird. I would have sworn that scream came from a woman's throat..."

John's comment caused Cruz—and about a dozen other by-standers—to erupt into laughter yet again.

Zhao, however, was stone-faced. John leaned in to ask him why he wasn't caught up in the others' giggle-fit.

"You know that O'Brien and I play cards fairly regularly, yes?" Zhao asked John.

John nodded.

"Well. Then it is safe to say that I know him more than most. And if there is one thing that I know about our friend O'Brien, it is that he is deathly supersti- tious. He claims that it is part of his Irish heritage—and I can neither confirm nor deny that. I have not had the pleasure of meeting many Irishmen—But what I can say with utmost certainty is that if O'Brien claims he saw a ghost... then O'Brien saw a ghost. It is not something he would say lightly."

Mr. Davis walked through the crowd, parting it like Moses did the Red Sea. The men—who were all chuckles moments before—suddenly sobered up at the sight of their foreman.

O'Brien struggled to light one of his Morley's. His fingers were trembling too much for him to properly work his butane lighter.

Mr. Davis, upon noticing this, took out his own lighter (a golden Zippo with his initials engraved in it, that cost more than John Henry and his crew would make in a year's worth of work) and lit O'Brien's cigarette for him.

"Much obliged, sir" O'Brien took a long drag and held it in his lungs for as long as he could before exhaling. "Cheers."

Mr. Davis nodded.

"Tell me what this is all about, son."

O'Brien nodded. He tried to steel his nerves, but his hands still shook.

"I saw somethin' movin' around. In the shadows, like."

"'Something? Or someone?"

O'Brien hesitated for a moment before he spoke.

"That's the thing, sir." O'Brien took another drag on his cigarette. "The ugly bugger was a wee bit of both."

The foreman leaned in and took a good whiff of O'Brien's breath.

"Mister O'Brien, have you been drinking?"

O'Brien smirked. "Are you asking me because I'm Irish?" O'Brien asked, leaning heavily into his accent. "Why, sir, that there is a harmful stereotype that has plagued my people ever since—"

Mr. Davis scowled. He stomped up to O'Brien and grabbed the Irishman by the throat with one hand. He rifled through O'Brien's pockets with his other hand. And he found a bottle. A whiskey bottle. And it was three-quarters empty.

Mr. Davis threw O'Brien to the ground.

"Oi! Watch it!" O'Brien shouted in protest.

"Yep. That's just what I figured," Mr. Davis said. He unscrewed the bottle of whiskey and poured what was left into the sand.

O'Brien jumped to his feet and balled his hands up into fists. "That doesn't belong to you, ya tosser. And neither do I. If a man wants to wet his whistle on his own time, that's his own bloomin' business."

John Henry stepped in and held O'Brien back, so he couldn't take a swing at the foreman.

Cruz and Zhao stepped out of the crowd and stood in front of Mr. Davis.

"Perhaps it's time we all returned to our quarters..." Zhao suggested.

"The sun does rise in a couple of hours," Cruz added.

Mr. Davis thought about it. After a few tense seconds, he conceded.

"Fine. Get back to your beds. I don't want anyone complaining tomorrow about not meeting their daily quota because they're tired."

John Henry slipped his arm underneath O'Brien's armpit and stabilized him so that he could walk in a straight line. "C'mon, pal" John said. "You can bunk with me tonight, in case that...thing... comes back."

O'Brien looked up at John with glassy eyes.

"So you believe me, then? You think I really did spot somethin' weird out there?"

"Sure," John lied. "Of course I do."

As John dragged O'Brien back to his campsite, he heard a sound he couldn't quite place. It was a cross between a meat tenderizer pounding into a slab of steak, and a child slurping a particularly saucy spaghetti noodle.

"FINE, GET BACK TO YOUR BEDS."

O'Brien's body tensed up. He dug his heels into the ground, doing his damnedest to make it difficult for John to keep dragging him along (this, of course, did nothing. John Henry was as strong as ten men and as stubborn as twenty. But he got the message just the same).

"Don't tell me you can't hear that?" O'Brien said, his lip trembling.

John Henry didn't answer. But he did let go of O'Brien.

Ol' John—as quietly as he could manage—scooped up the kerosene lamp he left burning from his date with Clementine earlier in the night. He tip-toed towards the source of the strange sound. Before shining the lamp at it, the silhouette of the shadow-drenched shape in front of John resembled that of a man hunched over, vomiting. Its shoulders heaved. Sick, wet, almost unnatural sounds escaped its throat.

But as soon as John's light hit the thing, it reacted as if it were being physically struck with a fist.

The sickly-pale creature spun around on its heels and stared at John with a deep hatred in its blood-red eyes. It screamed—and as it did so, something fell from its mouth. Something furry, and orange.

"Clementine!" John Henry yelled at the beast. "What in God's name have you done to Clementine?"

The monster yelled right back at John Henry—unhinging its jaw like a snake to allow more sound to escape its throat. John paid special attention to the creature's teeth—which resembled a kaleidoscope of knives; three rows of jagged, porcelain death.

The monster's back straightened, and it changed its entire silhouette. Its legs made sounds like the snapping of twigs as it stood up twice the height God intended it to be. It shoulder blades protruded from its back, ripping apart its flesh as well as it expanded, giving it the horrifying impression of tattered bat wings.

As monstrous as the thing appeared...John Henry couldn't help but shake the faint sense that he recognized it from somewhere.

As O'Brien tugged on John Henry's arm and begged him to "Run, you bleedin' idiot!" John squinted at the creature.

"...Big Al?" he asked.

Upon hearing its Christian name spoken aloud (or maybe it was just reacting to being spoken to at all?), the creature stopped screaming. Its shoulders fell. It cocked its head to the side, like a confused stray dog.

A sound emanated from its neck. It sounded not just painful...but difficult. Like it was trying to say something that its vocal chords were no longer in the proper shape to form.

John Henry watched, hypnotized by the sight of the thing. If it wasn't so horrifying, it'd be pitiful. This walking abomination, half-monster and half-man, was clearly a creature that nature never intended to exist. John Henry wasn't sure if he was just woozy from the adrenaline or not... but the monster's sheer presence seemed to wound the reality around it, making its immediate surroundings blurry and out-of-focus.

O'Brien was less intrigued by the fiend's presence than John. While the sight of beast sparked an intellectual curiosity in John Henry, it ignited a primal revulsion in O'Brien.

The panicked Irishman grabbed the kerosene lantern from John Henry's hand and hurled it at the monster with as much strength as his trembling arm could muster.

"No! Stop!" John Henry tried to yell—still enthralled by the monster's strange resemblance to his friend, Big Al.

But O'Brien couldn't hear John Henry's warning over the terrified pounding of his own heartbeat. "Burn, you devil!" O'Brien shouted.

As the lantern whipped towards the creature, it snapped back to its terrifying, mindless former state. It dodged the lantern so quickly, John Henry's eyes were unable to track it. The creature became a violent blur as it leaped into the air and retreated into the night.

But that doesn't mean that the danger was over. The lantern that O'Brien tossed, causing the creature to flee, smashed into a thick patch of creosote and ignited the moisture-starved creosote bush like it was a pile of tinder.

Coming face-to-face with a living demon felt surreal to John Henry, like something out of a nightmare. But a raging wildfire—especially one that threatened to spread to the campsite and burn alive everyone John knew—felt like a real, actual, real-world threat.

"Fire!" John yelled at the top of his lungs—but still unsure if his comrades at the other side of the camp would be able to hear him.

"'Out of the frying pan', as they say, eh?" O'Brien quipped. His voice cracked as he made the poorly-timed joke.

John Henry resisted the urge to reach out and strangle his Irish friend. He knew that inappropriate humor was just O'Brien's way of coping with how very serious their lives were, most of the time. But that knowledge didn't make it one lick less annoying.

"Help!" O'Brien screamed at the top of his lungs. "We got a fire here!"

"We can't just sit here and yell for help," John Henry noted. "By the time the cavalry arrives—if they ever do—the fire will have overtaken the entire campsite."

O'Brien looked around the campsite. "I don't know what you expect me to do," he said. "I don't have any water."

"Then we'll just have to improvise," O'Brien said as he grabbed a handful of sand and threw it at the growing flames.

John Henry quirked an eyebrow. "What was that supposed to do?"

"I dunno!" O'Brien yelled. "Smother it? I don't see you coming up with any bright ideas."

John took that as a challenge. He spun around on his heel and surveyed the campsite as quickly as he could, looking for anything that might help them smother the wall of flames that was steadily consuming every last cactus and patch of dry wood in its path.

His pile of old adventure magazines? Nope. That'd only make things worse.

The empty tin pot that John used to cook beans in, when he could afford them? Maybe if the fire was smaller, John could've used that to smother it. But we were already way past that point.

Then John's eyes settled on his trusty hammer. And he had an idea.

"What are ya gonna try an' do, knock the bloody thing out?" O'Brien asked as he saw John lifting his mighty mallet.

John was too focused on the task at hand to answer O'Brien's question. He focused all of his attention on leaping into the air, and slamming his hammer into the ground with such tremendous physical force that it left a meteor-sized crater in the ground and sent a tsunami of sand crashing towards the flames.

The sand did its job. It extinguished the flames entirely.

...So, when the foreman arrived with a cocked shotgun and a panicked look on his face, John Henry and O'Brien both looked like absolute fools.

"What? What's all the commotion about?"

John Henry and O'Brien share a look

"Um..." John Henry mumbled.

O'Brien just looked at the ground.

Mr. Davis looked right past John and stared daggers at O'Brien. "You, again?" the foreman screamed. "I thought I done told you to keep your nose clean!"

The foreman threw his shotgun down into the sand. But grabbed his left shirt cuff with his right hand and hurriedly rolled it up above his elbow. Then did the same thing with his left hand and his right sleeve.

The foreman's face burned so red, he looked like a human matchstick as he stomped towards O'Brien with his thick fingers balled up into fists.

"I knew I never should've hired no sheep-screwing Irishman to work the 'road'."

"Well, accept me apologies for not having the good fortune of being born south of the Mason-Dixon line. We can't all be fine, sister-diddling Southern Gentleman like yourself."

John Henry instinctively moved between the two men, and physically held them apart.

The foreman huffed and puffed and tried to brush past John Henry, but John just pressed his index and middle fingers into the man's solar plexus and held him still as a stone.

This, of course, embarrassed the foreman even more than O'Brien's verbal dig at his proud, Southern heritage.

"In my office! Now!" Mr. Davis bellowed. "The both of you!"

The foreman's "office" was actually a private train car. While his workers slept outside in the sand, Mr. Davis lived in luxury, in a personal chamber outfitted with its very own library, mini-bar, and coal stove.

Mr. Davis was a plain man, not overly fond of useless bric-a-brac cluttering up his space. But the one piece of decoration he did display, he did so proudly.

John Henry stared at the giant, tattered Confederate flag that Mr. Davis had framed above his desk. He tried his best not to... but the damned thing was directly in line-of-sight of the chair that the foreman offered to John Henry after he ushered them both into the car. Ol' John Henry was much too smart to assume that was a coincidence.

O'Brien sat on a short stool to John Henry's right. The foreman stood in front of them both, leaning against his desk with his arms folded, like a principal scolding two unruly children.

John Henry tried his best not to react to the flag. And he was no lightweight in the hiding-one's-emotions department. John Henry had years of experience concealing his inner world from masters and overseers who would take any glimmer of human emotion in his eyes as an excuse to wallop him within an inch of his natural-born life. But the thing was...despite his awesome, inexplicable strength... John was still only human. And sitting in the presence of the banner of the men who were willing to kill their own brothers for the right to legally own folks with the same color skin as him caused John Henry's left eye to rage-twitch ever-so-slightly.

Mr. Davis, because he was looking hard for it, noticed John Henry's visceral physical reaction to his flag.

"Ah," he said. "I see the old 'Stars and Bars' caught your eye. She's a beauty, ain't she?"

John Henry gritted his teeth so hard, you would've seen sparks if you peaked inside his cheeks. He gripped the armrests on his chair so tightly his thumbprints made deep, deep indentations in the wood.

"I see your frown. And I share your concern. Normally it'd be disrespectful to display a flag that isn't in the proper condition. But I prefer to think of her wear and tear as battle scars."

The foreman untucked his shirt to reveal a three-inch-long, diagonal shrapnel scar on his abdomen.

"But she's in good company, isn't she?"

John Henry stood up and pulled his shirt up over his head. He turned around, to show the foreman the latticework of whip scars that covered his back and broad shoulders.

"She sure is," John answered coldly.

The foreman gulped hard.

O'Brien—whose discomfort with the conversation had caused him to sober up considerably—faked a loud, rattling cough.

Both the foreman and John Henry turned their heads to glare at him.

"Gentlemen. Surely we're not here to pick at old scabs..." O'Brien said, attempting to change the subject as quickly as possible.

John Henry and the foreman locked eyes. After what seemed like hours (but, in reality, was actually around fourteen seconds) John Henry slid his shirt back on over his head, and took a seat.

The foreman cleared his throat.

"Well, then," he said, "Let's turn our attention to more current events. Specifically: why in the world I shouldn't fire you both for causing such a scene—or, make it two scenes—tonight?"

O'Brien was used to this kind of abusive behavior from the foreman. He, like the rest of the folks working for The Apache Railroad Company, had learned to swallow his pride and—

"I had a different subject in mind," John Henry interjected, interrupting O'Briens internal monologue...

The foreman stared daggers at John Henry.

O'Brien's jaw nearly hit the floor. In all the time he'd worked at The Kokopeli Express, he'd never heard someone talk back to the foreman so brazenly.

"In particular," John Henry went on, "I thought we could talk about what actually happened to Big Al."

All of the color—which wasn't much—drained from the foreman's face.

"C-can't say there's much to talk about..." the foreman stuttered in reply.

"You see, that's where you and I disagree," John Henry replied.

O'Brien stared at John, surprised by his friend's sudden boldness.

"I don't know if you are aware of this, but Big Al and I actually go back quite a few years."

"Is that right?" the foreman asked.

"It sure is, boss. And in all of that time, do you want to know what I never witnessed him do even once? I'm talking not a single time? Complain. About anything. And—believe you, me—I've seen him in some situations that you and your lily white skin could never, ever imagine..."

As soon as the foreman heard those last eight words, his "lily white skin" turned more of a candle-apple red. He stood up and banged his right fist against his oak desk so hard his middle knuckle split open and left a blood-stain upon the oak.

"Boy, you will show me the respect I am due or, with God as my witness, I'll—"

John Henry continued talking, as if the foreman hadn't uttered a word.

"...In fact, I'd need more than two hands to count the amount of times he has picked up the slack for me, personally. So I have a hard time believing the story you told us about him up and abandoning his post, leaving his fellow workers to account for his responsibilities. You want to fire me? Fine. I'll use my newfound spare time to walk my black ass into town and have a talk with the sheriff—and his beautiful new ebony wife—about Big Al's disappearance. And maybe I'll have enough oxygen in my lungs to talk a little about the working conditions around here, too"

"Yeah. Same here," O'Brien chimed in. "I mean... not the part about 'my black ass', obviously, but everythin' else. Especially the part about rattin' you out ta the proper authorities."

O'Brien winked at John Henry, and gave him the thumbs up.

John Henry smiled.

The foreman seethed with anger.

All three men sat in tense silence for a few moments. O'Brien discreetly reached into his pocket and palmed his lucky bottle opener, in case a fight broke out and he needed to cheat.

Luckily, he wouldn't have to. The foreman sighed and pointed at the door.

"You two ugly bastards get out of my sight," he growled.

John Henry stood and made his way towards the door. "Gladly," he said.

O'Brien curtsied towards the foreman. "Have a lovely rest of your evenin'," he said. And then he followed John Henry out the door.

As John and O'Brien exited the foreman's train car, they were ambushed by Zhao and Cruz, who were waiting impatiently for them outside. Cruz was the first to pipe up.

"You guys were in there forever!" he said. "We were gonna wait five more minutes, and if you didn't come out we were gonna kick the door down and swoop in for the rescue."

Zhao nodded. "As always, our esteemed colleague exaggerates. But it is true that we were concerned. Are you gentlemen alright?"

"And, more importantly, are you still proud employees of The Apache Railroad Company?"

"Aye," O'Brien answered. "You haven't gotten rid of us just yet."

John Henry smiled and patted Cruz on the back so hard he accidentally knocked the wind out of the man.

Zhao looked to John. "We were all the way across the campsite when we heard you yell for help. By the time we made it over to where you were, the two of you ere already gone. All that was left was a crater, some scorched earth, and a pile of white ash."

"What was it that startled you, big guy?" Cruz asked John Henry. He tried to conjure up an image of what it would take to strike fear into the heart of "The Steel-Working Super-Man", and he shuddered at the blood-curdling vision his subconscious provided for him.

John Henry looked down at the ground. "Nothing," he mumbled. "Just a shadow."

Cruz and Zhao shared a skeptical glance. They weren't buying it.

O'Brien gave John Henry a few more seconds to walk back his "shadow" comment explain himself properly. When he didn't take the opportunity to do so, O'Brien just couldn't hold back any longer.

"A bleedin' Boogeyman, is what it was!" O'Brien exclaimed. Eleven feet tall, if it was an inch. Half bat, half wolf, half gorilla. With fangs like a pair of Bowie knives. And eyes as red as the devil's bollocks. Slurping up blood like it was his Sunday mornin' biscuits and gravy".

Cruz chuckled nervously. "Sure. Right. And this devil just let the two of you go?"

"Obviously not," O'Brien answered. "He flew away, didn't he?"

"Oh. Right. I should have guessed," Cruze rolled his eyes.

Zhao quirked an eyebrow. "Half bat, half wolf, half gorilla?"

O'Brien was starting to get red in the face. "That's right."

"Don't you think that's one half too many?" Zhao asked.

O'Brien turned to John Henry. He didn't say anything out loud. But the exasperated expression on his face positively screamed "little help?"

John Henry sighed.

"He's not lying," John said. Even though he knew how ridiculous that sounded. "And he's not drunk. Or, I mean, not any more drunk than he usually is.."

O'Brien did a little Irish jig and took an exaggerated bow.

"We saw...something...out there," John Henry continued. "Something inhuman."

An uncomfortable silence held in the air.

"I know it sounds crazy..." John said. "But it was real. And it... it got Clementine."

Cruz's shoulders fell. "Oh, man" he said. "Not our Clemmy..."

"Your story doesn't sound as crazy as you might think" said "Zhao. "Not exactly. Every culture on Earth has stories about blood-drinking monsters. In China, we have 'the Jiangshi'—reanimated corpses who pounce on the living, in order to steal their 'chi', or 'life force'."

"That's what I'm saying!" O'Brien exclaimed, excited. "Me nan used to scare the bejesus out of me and mine with stories o' the 'The Abhartach'—an Irish monster who could only be killed by running him through with a sword made of yew, burying the bugger upside-down, and surrounding his grave with a bush o' thorns."

"That seems like a lot," Cruz said.

"Hey, brother—if you saw what old John and me saw back there, you'd take the extra precautions too."

Cruz thought about it. "I've never seen one myself, of course...but my dad was a ranchero. And he claimed that two summers before I was born, our livestock was terrorized by what the locals called 'el chupacabra'—or, 'the goatsucker': A mangy creature with glowing eyes and a hypodermic needle for a tongue."

John shook his head. "Whatever we saw, it's gone now. If we're lucky, the damn thing took its belly full of blood into a cave somewhere and is hibernating for the next hundred years."

"And if we're not so lucky?" Cruz asked.

"Then I suppose it'll come back and do to us what it did to Big Al" O'Brien answered.

Cruz, Zhao, and John Henry each looked at one another and winced. They were both thinking that exact same thought...but of the four of them, only O'Brien was tactless enough to say it out loud.

John Henry didn't speak up. He didn't tell them that he recognized a flash of Big Al's presence in the monster's eyes. And he sure as Hell didn't share anything about the pitiful, confused the sound it made when John Henry referred to it by Big Al's name. No. Instead of disclosing those pieces of information, John Henry simply balled up his fist and punched the foreman's train car so hard his fist left a dent in the steel.

Zhao walked over to John and placed a hand on the man's heaving shoulder. "There's nothing we can do about it now, John," Zhao said. "The best thing we can do is get some sleep, so we that we are rested and ready for when it returns."

John Henry didn't say anything in response. He simply walked towards his tent. He doubted he would get any sleep that night. Or ever again, for that matter.

✝✝✝

The next morning, John Henry, O'Brien, Cruz, and Zhao met at the tracks where they left off the previous work day. Both John Henry and O'Brien had their hammers slung over their respective shoulders. Zhao carried the massive metal spike. Cruz had on a backpack full of dynamite.

No one said anything about the night before. All of them—tired as dogs—simply nodded at each other and got down to business.

Usually they talked a lot (especially O'Brien, and Cruz). Topics ranged from whose culture had the best looking women, to who would win in a fight between Jax Meteor and The Shadow. Today? Nothing. Dead silence. Nothing but the sound of steel hammering against steel.

Which is what made it possible for the men to hear the soft meowing of something hiding in the shadows of a patch of desert milkweed.

"Clemmy!" Cruz shouted, with an even mixture of surprise and relief in his voice. He practically dove into the brush to retrieve the gang's presumed-fallen feline friend.

Zhao turned to John Henry and squinted. "I thought you said Clementine was devoured by whatever beast you and O'Brien claim to have encountered last night.

"She was," John Henry answered. "I don't know what cat that is, but she sure ain't—"

"John?" O'Brien asked. His voice wavered. And as soon as John Henry got a good look at what O'Brien's eyes were fixed on, he understood why.

The orange and brown fur. The missing left eye. The jagged, lightning-bolt-shaped chunk out of her right ear... it was Clemmy, alright. There absolutely no mistaking it.

"Well, I'll be a monkey's uncle," John Henry gasped. "It's her".

And it was. But there was something wrong.

Clementine, who was usually as social as any cat has ever been, hissed at Cruz as he attempted to coax her out from within the shade of the flower patch.

But Cruz wouldn't take "no" for an answer.

...AND GOT DOWN TO BUSINESS.

"It's okay, mija," Cruz whispered as he reached in to grab her.

But it wasn't okay. Clementine hissed again. And then she sank her teeth—which seemed not only much sharper, but much largely than they used to be—into the soft webbing between Cruz's thumb and forefinger.

"Clem!" John Henry shouted. "That ain't like you at all!"

Cruz swore in Spanish and yanked his hand out of the bush. But little Clementine didn't ease her up on her grip one little bit. Her teeth stayed locked into his hand, even as he swung her over his head.

Even when her skin made contact with the sunlight and she burst into flames, little Clementine didn't let go. In fact, Zhao burned his palms mighty fierce as he leaped in without thinking, yanked Clementine's flaming body off of Cruz, and slammed her into the sand.

Clementine yowled in pain. She was charred to a crisp—like a piece of overcooked bacon—but her furious hissing gave off the impression that she was more angry than injured.

John Henry picked up his hammer. His eyes welled up with tears.

"I'm sorry, Clemmy..." he whispered.

Then he brought the head of his hammer down onto her skull with such tremendous force, her body exploded into a cloud of bone fragments, cinders, and ash.

John and the rest of the men stood there in dumbfounded silence.

After two long minutes, O'Brien was the first one to speak.

"Jesus, Mary, and Joseph!" he exclaimed.

"Yep," said John Henry. "That about sums it up."

O'Brien turned to Cruz and Zhao. "Are you fellas alright?" he asked.

Zhao turned his palms outward.

John Henry winced at the sight of them. He hadn't seen burns that bad since his old life, when his master's wife threw her wedding ring into a bonfire after a fight with her husband, and John's master commanded one of John Henry's fellow slaves to fetch it out of the embers while they still burned bright orange.

O'Brien made a sympathetic sound.

"How about you, Cruz?" O'Brien asked. "Looked like ol' Clemmy took a real serious bite out of ya."

Cruz showed then men his hand. The two puncture marks in his hand from where Clementine had bitten him were still bleeding heavily.

John—whose altruistic instincts compelled him to ease suffering wherever he saw it—immediately stepped forward, ripped a strip of cloth from the left sleeve of his shirt, and used the impromptu towel to wipe down Cruz's wound.

Once the blood was wiped away, John and the ret of the men could see that all of the veins leading up to the holes were black and raised. They looked like converging streets on a map of the city.

O'brien stepped up and examined the wound.

"You ever seen anything like that?" John asked.

"Once. Coworker of mine bot bitten by a rattlesnake. Had an irrational fear o' the doctor, and let it go untreated for the better part of a week. It looked... better than that." O'Brien said.

"We should into town," said Zhao

"I'm fine," said Cruz. "Far less sturdy men have withstood far more serious—" but, before he could finish his sentence, Cruz passed out from a mixture of pain and lack of blood.

Mr. Davis sat in his private train car, pouring himself an obscenely full glass of top-shelf brandy when someone knocked on his door with such tremendous force; it threatened to knock the car off the rails.

The foreman opened the door, and saw that it was John Henry knocking. Though, he probably could have guessed that before opening the door. It was either him knocking, or six men with a battering ram.

Behind John, O'Brien was pushing an unconscious Cruz in a wheelbarrow. Zhao stood beside him, with both hands wrapped in bandages that appeared to be fashioned from bits of John's torn t-shirt.

"Something happened to Cruz," John said.

"Something weird," said O'Brien. "Really, really weird."

Zhao approached the foreman respectfully, as he always did. And the foreman appreciated him for that. Out of all of the men he employed, Zhao was the one the foreman wanted to strangle the least.

"Sir," Zhao started. "My colleagues and I apologize for bothering you at this hour. But we need to take Cruz into town, for medical attention. He has been... poisoned. Bitten by a sick animal. It may be rabies. Or it may be...something else."

The foreman waited a few seconds before he spoke. If it was anyone but Zhao asking him help, he would have told them to go jump in a ditch, and fill it full of sand after they had. But Mr. Davis had always kind of liked Zhao. Sure, he was a "slippery oriental", but he was quiet. And well-mannered. And seemed to know his place. As far as the foreman could see it, the only serious character flaw Zhao had was that he mixed it up with poor company. But you can hardly blame a man for that, way out here. There weren't many companions to pick from.

"Town's a good twenty miles away," the foreman grunted.

"That's exactly why we came to you," Zhao answered. "We were wondering if, respectfully—"

"Enough with the bleedin' pleasantries!" O'Brien blurted out. "Your horse! We need ta borrow your stupid horse, or else Cruz here is going to drift into the big, final sleep before we make it to the medic."

John Henry cleared his throat. He knew that what he was about to ask was a long-shot, but he said it with as much calm and conviction as he could muster. "And we need you to cut our paychecks early. So we have enough to pay the doc."

The foreman shook his head.

"No. Ain't no way in God's green earth I'm giving you a sack of money, and loaning you my personal steed, so you can run off in the middle of the night and..." The foreman stopped speaking, and squinted at Cruz.

"Is that boy even sick? Or could it be that maybe you three hooligans were just celebrating after a long day of barely-doing-any-work, and he tied one on a little too tight?"

The foreman was on a roll, now. One of the old man's greatest talents was, when he didn't want to do the right thing, convincing himself that it was actually everyone else around him who was trying to cheat, confuse, and betray him and not the other way around.

"No, no—," the foreman continued. "I've got it. This is all a scam, isn't it? The second I open my safe to slide you your earnings, you boys put a pistol to my dome and clean me out for all I'm worth. Well, no sirree. Foreman Jefferson Davis might've been born yesterday, but he stayed up all night. And—"

John Henry pulled his work hammer from his belt and used the wooden handle to tap the foreman on the forehead as gently as he could manage, with his nigh-superhuman strength.

It knocked the foreman out cold.

Zhao couldn't believe what he saw. He dove towards the foreman and caught his limp body before his head connected with the ground.

"John!" Zhao shouted. "What in the world have you done?"

John used his hammer to gesture towards Cruz, who was groaning, sweating and writhing in pain in the wheelbarrow.

"O'Brien is right. This ain't no kind of time to be polite. We're running out of time. A man's life is at stake."

Zhao threw his hands up in defeat.

"I am done," Zhao said.

Zhao turned, and patted Cruz on the knee.

"John, O'Brien, Cruz—you three have behaved as brothers towards me since I took this job. And I deeply appreciate that. But, as you know, I do have a real family. That is the reason I took this job. To make money, that I can send back to them, to make their lives easier."

Zhao kneeled next to the unconscious foreman and placed a hand on his chest, to make sure he was still breathing.

"But, after this, there is no way the foreman will let me keep working. Hell, I will be lucky if he doesn't have me deported."

Zhao sighed. And shook his head.

"This is ridiculous. I did not come to America to fool around with evil spirits and get mixed up in the assault and battery of a rich white man."

Zhao walked over to where the foreman's horse, "Palomino Lightning", was hitched. He untied the horse's reigns from the pole and hopped on its back.

John Henry and O'Brien looked at each other as Zhao rode off into the horizon..

"Did that wily Chinese bastard just steal our only way back to town?" O'Brien asked.

"I believe he did," John Henry answered. "I believe he did."

✝✝✝

John Henry and O'Brien each held one handle of the wheelbarrow as they pushed the rolling hunk of rusted metal—with Cruz in it—through the desert. But, in O'Brien's case, it was mostly for show.

Case in-point: John paused for a moment to wipe the sweat from his brow, and O'Brien—who was leaning on the wheelbarrow just to keep himself upright—tipped the whole contraption over, and spilled Cruz's unconscious body into the sand.

"Whoa!" John dropped to his knee and caught Cruz before his head connected with the hard ground. "Maybe we should set up camp for the night," John Henry suggested.

"Yeah. That might be a good idea," O'Brien said sheepishly.

No longer required to stand, O'Brien promptly allowed himself to collapse onto the ground. He watched as John Henry gently lifted Cruz's unconscious body back into the wheelbarrow, and laid him down to rest. Cruz's normally-bronze skin had turned paper-white. His veins were raised and black, like they were passing tar instead of blood. His breath was shallow, and rattled in his lungs as it escaped his mouth.

O'Brien shook his head. "If this poor bastard survives the night, it'll be an

outright miracle. "John..." O'Brien's voice cracked. "I know you're only pausing to rest on my account. And I sure as Hell appreciate the sentiment. But I
don't reckon ol' Cruz has the time to spare. If we want Cruz to see tomorrow,
you better leave me be and power on through the night."

John Henry didn't want to hear them, but as soon as the words hit John
Henry's ears, he knew they were nothin' but true.

Their only chance was to leave O'Brien in the desert—to fend for himself
against the cold, the coyotes, and whatever other dangers lurked out there—
while John Henry schlepped through the night by himself, and delivered
Cruz's body to the town doc as quickly as humanly possible.

"But what about—" John Henry started to say. But O'Brien stopped him
before he could continue.

"Don't pay no mind to me, boy-o. No reason to worry," O'Brien lied. "I'll be
just fine out here."

O'Brien, exhausted beyond words, lied down flat on the dust and closed his
led-heavy eyelid. "Just need to rest my eyes a bit and I'll catch up with you in
two shakes of an Englishman's wife's tail."

O'Brien nodded grimly. He was unsure if he was trading one friend's life
for another. But there was thing on which he was damn sure: if O'Brien died
out here in the dark, it wasn't going to be in vain. John Henry would get Cruz
into town by the sunrise, come Hell or high water.

"Take care of yourself, O'Brien," John Henry said.

"Don't have too much of a choice now, do I?" O'Brien quipped.

John Henry pressed on.

✝✝✝

Two solid hours of uninterrupted walking later, John noticed that his shoes
had begun to squeak. Worried that the sound was going to draw unnecessary
attention from nocturnal desert predators, he paused for a second to empty
the sweat from his overworked work boots.

But it wasn't sweat that filled John Henry's shoes. It was blood—shed from
the soles of his feet, which had been rubbed raw from stomping through the
hot sand for well over six hours.

As soon as the first drop of blood hit the sand, John Henry heard an unholy scream ring through the night—followed by the sound of heavy, leathery
wings flapping furiously. And closer, closer, closer—until the creature they be-
longed to—the massive bat-like-creature who John Henry had caught preying
on Clementine much earlier in the night.

Out here, under the clear light of the moon, John Henry could make the creature out a lot more easily. In particular: its facial features. And the telltale "X" shaped scar scratched onto the right side of its face. There was no use trying to deny it. This thing was—or, at least, used to be—Big Al.

As the monster swooped down towards John Henry, John noticed that it was moving more erratically before. Like it was operating more on base instinct, rather than any kind of human intelligence. Before, when he caught the creature feeding on Clementine, it was hunched over in the dark—it looked embarrassed to be feeding on her. Ashamed, even.

But now, the scent of human blood had whipped the creature into a frenzy that—even for someone as physically capable as John Henry—was downright terrifying.

"Hang on, Cruz" John Henry whispered to his barely-unconscious friend, as he gripped the wheelbarrow by both its handles.

Cruz stirred semi-awake. He blinked at John Henry through his delirium and asked "Whazzapening, amigo? Are we goin' for a ride?"

"Yep," John Henry answered. And he shoved the wheelbarrow with all his considerable might, sending it rolling deep into the darkness, and (hopefully) out of harm's way.

The monster was almost on top of John Henry now. As it reached tout o grasp John Henry's throat, the digits in its fingers popped. The skin peeled back on the tips of its fingers, to reveal talons that were sharper than a mother-in-law's tongue.

John grabbed the hammer from its loop on his belt and swung it for all he was worth at the blood-thirsty monster that was screaming its lungs out as it barreled down on him.

"I don't know if there's anything left in there that can hear me," John Henry said. "But I am real sorry about this." And he meant it. It seemed to John Henry like there was nothing left of the honorable man that he once knew left inside that penny-dreadful monster. And that meant that his responsibilities now entirely lied with protecting Cruz—who hadn't yet crossed the line into full-blown-monster territory.

It turned out, John Henry had nothing to be sorry for. The creature-who-used-to-be-Big-Al had gotten much more comfortable piloting his new vessel in the hours since it and John last tussled. The unholy beast twisted its body out of the path of John's hammer. It hovered in the air for just a moment, and then dive-bombed towards John Henry's mallet and clasped its handle with both its gnarled feet.

John applied the entirety of his considerable strength to the problem of yanking that hammer back. But it just wouldn't budge. Not even an inch.

While John Henry's weird strength was always more than a match for any man he ever came across—this thing was something else. Something more than a man. Or perhaps something considerably less. Either way: it was strong as Hell (perhaps, literally). Strong enough to wrench the hammer from John Henry's grasp and hurl it deep into the dessert.

This, understandably, stunned John Henry. In all his years on Earth, John had never met an opponent strong enough to separate him from his signature weapon. Now that he was without it, John Henry felt...wrong. Like King Arthur without Excalibur, Poseidon without his Trident, or Jax Meteor without his quartet of ray guns.

But just because he lost his weapon, didn't mean he lost his fighting spirit. John Henry did what any man worth his salt does in a desperate, no-win scenario: he sucked it up, dug his heels into the dirt, and raised his fists.

"I'm sorry for what happened to you. I truly am," John said. "But losing one friend is enough. I won't let you take Cruz too."

The sinister specimen rocketed towards John Henry with unholy speed, mouth open and row, after row, after row of jagged teeth glinting in the moonlight.

John Henry formed a cross with his forearms in front of his face, slammed his eyelids shut, dugs his feet into the sand, and braced for impact.

But, lucky for him, that impact never came.

Because, right out from behind John Henry, a monstrous figure leaped out of the shadows and whacked the creature-who-used-to-be-Big-Al with a wheelbarrow so hard, the thing rang like a bell for a good ten seconds afterward.

John Henry—who was shocked to find out he hadn't been reduced to a fine red mist by his enemy's teeth and talons—slowly opened his eyes. And what he saw made his heart sink down deep into his belly.

John Henry's old buddy Cruz had jumped up from the wheelbarrow John left him in and was sprinting at full-speed towards his opponent.

Only, Cruz wasn't quite Cruz anymore. John Henry's amigo had begun to transform into some kind of supernatural entity, the same way Big Al had... Only, instead of adopting the qualities of a bat (the wings, the pointy ears, etcetera), Cruz had morphed into something every bit as bloodthirsty, but more cat-like in its appearance—some kind of feline fiend. He even had the beginnings of a tail sprouting out the back of his overalls.

"Go!" the-thing-that-used-to-be-Cruz growled. "Get into town before the sun falls. I'll hold him off."

John Henry tried his damndest to obey Cruz's orders. But, try as he might, he just couldn't get his feet to obey his brain. Instead, he watched in stunned horror as his two former-friends-turned-monsters became a tangle of teeth of claws. He clasped his hands around his ears as the once-peaceful desert soundscape erupted into a cacophony of nightmarish screams, growls and the sickly-wet sound of live meat being shaved off of bone.

"I said...go!" Cruz shouted again. And John could tell that it took every ounce of willpower for Cruz to summon the humanity necessary to form the words. The poor bastard's throat just wasn't in the shape to make human sounds anymore.

John didn't have to be told a third time. He ran.

And the-thing-that-was-Cruz continued to fight. But its movements were glacial and awkward compared to its bat-like opponent. Whereas Cruz had only been an abomination for minutes, the bat had been a monster for hours— which gave him the edge, when it came to one-on-one combat experience.

The bloodthirsty cat's claws clashed with the parasite-bat's talons. They bit at each others necks, and screamed-cursed from newly-mutated vocal chords as they tumbled through the sand.

Until, eventually, the bat-creature realized that wrestling on the ground with a cat the size of railway hand was a fool's errand, when you had wings that'd make a pterodactyl's eyes green with envy.

The bat creature dug its claws deep into Cruz-the-cat-creature's armpits and used its obscenely powerful haunches to launch them both high into the night sky.

And without any the ground beneath its feet to use as leverage, Cruz-the-cat-creature scrambled in a mad panic to try to find any way to wrestle with the bat.

And while Cruz-the-cat-creature scrambled, the bat took bite, after bite, after bite out of its neck and shoulders—watering the cacti below with feline fiend's cursed blood.

The sudden loss of blood, combined with the thinning atmosphere as the bat creature continued its ascent, caused the-creature-who-used-to-be-Cruz's thoughts to become cloudy and sluggish. It could feel the life steadily draining from its newly-cursed form, and—for a quick second—it thought, "good".

...But then the-creature-who-used-to-be-Cruz thought of what would happen once he died. The creature would go after John Henry. And that was something Cruz just couldn't allow. Despite their differences in skin color, age, and station, John Henry had never been anything except warm and generous Cruz. When Cruz was too exhausted to hold his spike straight, John Henry offered to hold it for him. On the rare occasion Cruz was late to the job, ol' John Henry covered for him with the boss. When Cruz received the telegram that his mother had passed away, and he wandered out in the desert to get blind drunk and cry his eyes out where the other men couldn't see him, John was the only one who sat up all night waiting for him to return.

And Cruz would be Heaven scorned if he would let the man down now... cat creature or not.

Cruz summoned what was left of his strength into his increasingly-fury arms and swiped his claws across the bat monster's wings.

Against the insane, unnatural sharpness of Cruz's claws, the bat creature's wings tore like wet tissue paper. The bat creature screamed in a mixture of pain and shock as both he and his giant cat quarry began to plummet towards the sand.

Cruz, rather predictably because of his new form, landed on his feet.

The bat, however, met a different fate. Specifically: he fell, heart-first, onto the splintered wooden handle of John Henry's broken mallet.

"Goodnight, Big Al" John said. Instead of running into town when Cruz told him to, he ran towards his hammer. And, after watching the monsters' aerial battle closely, he positioned himself in the perfect spot to impale the bat monster as it fell.

Having witnessed little Clementine's fiery demise firsthand, John Henry knew what to expect when Big Al drew his last breath. He charged at Cruz-the-cat-creature and tackled him like a linebacker, knocking them both behind a nearby boulder.

Big Al's vampiric corpse exploded with such explosive power, it rivaled the sound of the dynamite John Henry and his crew used to clear a path for the railway. The resultant flash was so bright; it turned the night as bright as early morning for just a moment, and caused the-creature-who-used-to-be-Cruz to wince. Most of the creature's body was instantly turned into a slurry of pink gore, but one of its rib bones was propelled away from its body with such force, it embedded itself four inches deep into the rock behind which John Henry was hiding.

John Henry turned to the-creature-who-used-to-be-Cruz. Its chest was still rising and falling—but its inhalations were shallow, and its exhalations were accompanied by a slight pained whimper.

John patted the monster's chest. "Let's just lay here a while, buddy. Take a load off. You earned it."

John Henry looked over his shoulder at the horizon, and counted down the seconds until the sun rose.

†††

"GOOD NIGHT, BIG AL."

Hours later, the vibration of horse hooves and the sound of excited laughter caused John Henry to stir back to consciousness.

Before investigating the source of the sounds, John turned to look over at Cruz. There was nothing left of his old friend except for a smoking hold in the ground, and a couple fists' worth of ashes.

"Aw, Cruz..." John Henry said aloud. Silently, he said a prayer that his friend's soul found its way to Heaven, despite the whole "monster" thing there at the end.

The laughter and the clip-clop of horseshoes grew closer.

"John?" a voice half-yelled, half-laughed. "John Henry? Is that you?"

John sat up with a start.

Looming over him was Zhao, on the foreman's horse, with O'Brien sat behind him.

"How did you find me?" John Henry asked, not believing his luck.

O'Brien chuckled and gestures with his thumb towards the mile-long trail blood and chunks of gore that led towards John Henry's resting place. Strings of far-flung intestine hung from patches of cacti like strings of garland from a Christmas tree.

"Oh," John Henry said. "I see."

He turned to Zhao, and smiled. "I knew you'd never make it far. You took three steps towards town and you turned right back around to make sure ol' O'Brien and I were okay, didn't you? You talk like your heart's made of stone, but you're as big and soft as the foreman's mattress aren't you?"

Zhao spit on the sand. "Hell no. I made it into town...," Zhao looked down at the ground. A dark shadow fell across his face. "...but the vampire bat that bit Cruz got there first. And it sunk its teeth into better'n half the town by the time I got there. I barely made it out in once piece. As I ran out of town with my tail tucked squarely between my legs, I bumped into O'Brien, who was trying to make his way in."

O'Brien waved to John Henry from the back of the horse. "Hiya, John."

"Hey, O'Brien" John Henry returned his little wave. "I see you're feeling much better."

"I am!" O'Brien pulled a three-quarters-empty glass bottle of whiskey from his boot and hoisted it proudly over his head. "Zhao brought me back some medicine from town!'

"Cruz didn't make it, huh?" Zhao gestured to the bloodstained, scorch-marked crater that John Henry stood next to.

"I'm afraid not, pal" John Henry replied.

"Yeah...I figured as much" Zhao sighed. "First Big Al, then Cruz...only the three of us remain."

A long, heavy silence held in the air for what seemed like hours—but was, in actuality, probably just a solid minute.

John Henry looked at his friends. "You know we have to go back into that town, you just came from right?"

O'Brien hopped off the horse. He stomped towards John Henry with his hands raised, palms out.

"John, no. Just...no. I know you're always 'Mr. Do the Right Thing', but what you're talking about is suicide, man!"

Zhao nodded his head in agreement. "John, we barely made it out of this mess with our lives. It's a miracle we're still standing. And how you want us to rush headfirst into certain doom of our own accord? That's like spitting in God's face for sparing our souls."

John Henry looked at Zhao. "You said the town was *half* transformed into those monsters. *Half.* That means that half its people—a considerable amount of which I assumed are women and children—are just sitting around like lambs before the slaughter..."

Zhao and O'Brien were both silent. They knew that John Henry was right. And, more than that, they knew that there was no use trying to talk John Henry out of something once he set his mind to it. If there was once force stronger than that of his mighty hammer swing, it was the force of his convictions. And the thing about being around a man with convictions as powerful as John Henry's was that it was every bit as infectious as a vampire's bite.

After a long time, O'Brien spoke up. "Alright. Let's say ol' Zhao and I were dumb enough to follow you into Hell. What are the three of us supposed to do against a horde of undead, blood-gulping monsters?"

✝✝✝

It turned out that killing vampires wasn't too different from steel-driving work. It was still basically a three-man job. One of them (Zhao, usually, because he was the best grappler of the three—due to a bit of childhood-dabbling in the martial arts) had to wrestle the demon to the ground. Another had to hold a spike over its heart ("these monsters sure squirm more than the stone we're used to working with," O'Brien quipped), and another (John Henry) to hammer the stake so hard it cleaved the creature's unnaturally strong skin, ribcage, and heart in a single strike.

Once they got the rhythm of it, John Henry and the boys found they could put down a couple of vampires an hour—especially since they worked during the day, when the creatures were at their physically weakest and most vulnerable.

After three long days (and even longer nights), they had cleared the town of its vampire infestation, and made it safe for the uninfected to emerge from their boarded-up cellars and church basements, to resume the lives that God intended for them.

By that time, John Henry and the gang had heard whispers of the next town that was torn asunder by the vampire curse. So they hopped on horseback and made their way over.

And once they cleaned that town out, they moved onto the next, and the next. Until they eventually tracked down the bat who started the whole mess and ground the poor, cursed creature into dust.

Following the trail of dead (and the undead) across the sands of the Sonora ate up the last of their Summer. The trio split up for the winter and found themselves working for different railroads. None of them ever spoke to anyone else about the time they spent hammering hunks of hickory into the unbeating hearts of the damned.

But John Henry carried the weight of that season in his own heart for the rest of his life...which wasn't to be a whole Hell of a lot longer...

✝✝✝

After having witnessed two of his friends transmogrify into blood-hungry enemies of God and then explode into ash in the light of the sun, John Henry promised himself that, at his next gig, he would lay low, and keep to his own self as much as was physically possible. "No more excitement," he promised himself. "No more adventures." Which is pretty darn funny, if you ask me. 'Cause, the story of John Henry's next Summer, every man, woman, and child in The West knows.

Eager for a fresh start in a brand spankin' new locale, John Henry left the Southwest for good. Ironically, his job forging American's railways didn't pay well enough for him to afford a ticket on one of the trains that traveled atop them. (And even if it had, he'd have to suffer the indignity of riding in one of the "Blacks-only" coach cars, which weren't fit to transport cattle, let along a sovereign human being). So he made like a common hobo, and hitched rides in whatever relatively-empty boxcars he could find.

John Henry had more than a few close-calls "riding the rails". Between the literal snarling watchdogs and their overzealous railroad police masters, ol' John had to make sure he always kept his head on a well-greased swivel. But he made do. And when he eventually wound up halfway across the country, in West Virginia, he found hammer-swingin' work in The Chesapeake and Ohio

Railroad Company, helping to blast a tunnel clear through The Allegheny Mountains.

John Henry minded his own darn business with such a monastic discipline, a rumor circulated 'round his new colleagues that he was either hard-of-hearing, or slow-of-brain. Or, possibly, both. All anyone knew about the man was what they could see with their own two (or however many God saw fit to give them) eyes. And that's that he was a hard worker; and a man of utmost personal integrity. He was never late, often early, never left his chores for another man, and never complained when another man left their chores for him.

But this was gettin' to be late into the 1880's—when the automated steel drill had begun to come into fashion, putting steel-driving men all over the country out of work, whether they had a butt-load of integrity or not.

Thankfully, John Henry's new foreman ("Mr. Everett"—not that his name matters much) was nothing like his old one, Mr. Davis. When a city-boy with a smooth voice an even smoother hands paid The Chesapeake and Ohio Railroad Company a visit, trying to tell them how they should conduct their business, the new foreman at least had enough decency in him to offer the crew a chance to save their skins, if they were brave enough to take it. Namely: the foreman gave his word as a white, Christian man that, if any of the men on his payroll could best the soulless new machine in a race, he'd box the automaton back up and keep the paychecks flowing for at least one more season.

Of course, when time came to pick out their champion, every single eyeball in the camp turned and fell squarely on John Henry's beautiful, bald, black head.

John Henry, of course, at first, didn't want anything to do with any kind of big to-do like that. A high-profile challenge like that sure violated his personal "No more excitement, no more adventures" policy. But, still, John Henry couldn't find it in himself to just say "no". Not just because it was the right thing to do (even though it was). Or because he didn't want to disappoint his fellow rail workers (even though he didn't). It was because, when John Henry laid his eyes on that infernal machine, he didn't see just another mundane tangle of oil and iron...he saw yet another Gosh dang monster trying to imitate and replace humanity.

John Henry agreed to race the machine one-on-one the following morning, for the honor of every rail worker who came before him, and the fate of every one who hoped to come after him.

✝✝✝

The next day, as John Henry strolled up to the worksite where he was to compete against that accursed machine, his heart sank. Not because he was scared (he wasn't) but because he saw the crowd of the folks who had assembled to watch him.

Apparently, the smooth-talking son-of-a-gun whose job it was to sell automated steel drills to every penny-pinching foreman in The Southwest Territories had heard about the wager the foreman had made with John Henry, and he—so confident in his contraption's certain victory, he was—alerted the local press-types.

John Henry sneezed as the sulfurous smoke of an exploding flash-bulb overwhelmed his olfactory senses. Instead of doing the decent thing and saying "God bless you", a reporter shouted "Mister John Henry! What do you think the odds are that you'll beat the automatic drill?"

"Don't you think it's a little...arrogant...of you to think you can do better than a machine?" Another reporter asked, looking down his nose.

John Henry didn't answer either of them. He knew that nothing he could say would satisfy either of them. Besides, they probably both typed up the articles they wanted to write before they even showed up to watch him race.

No, John Henry didn't take note of any of the reporters who were there to record his downfall that morning. But what he did pay attention to a couple of little boys in the front row (one white and one black. Not that it matters, none. But it does...), who had brought their own handmade "Good luck John Henry!" sign.

John dropped to one knee, so that he was eye-level with the kids as he spoke to them.

"Do your daddies know you're here?"

"Mine gave me the shoe polish we used to make the sign," the white boy answered.

"And yours?" John Henry asked the other.

The black child nodded. "My daddy works with you," he replied.

John blinked hard. "Well. I guess I had better win this race then. So's we still have a job to go to in the morning."

The kids both nodded in unison.

The photographer snapped another photo of John, this time of all three of them.

"Give 'em Hell, John Henry!" a man in the crowd cheered. Then another. Then another.

Before long, it looked like everyone assembled was clapping and hollering, letting our hero know just where they stood in the whole "man-vs.-machine" debate.

As John Henry walked towards the starting line of the contest, the crowd's cheers were like having the wind blowing on your back during a foot race. He felt lighter, stronger (which was really saying something), lifted up by an invisible force that was not his own.

It wasn't a bad feeling. Especially not for a former slave.

"Life sure is damn strange..." John Henry muttered under his breath to no one in particular. But the corners of his mouth were turned upwards when he said it.

John nodded respectfully at the drill salesman, who stood behind his metal monstrosity. The armpits of his hundred dollar suit were stained with sweat. He dabbed his forehead with a silk pocket square that probably cost more than everything John Henry owned, all added up together.

"I hope you don't mind me saying so, sir," John Henry said, "but you look a little warm this morning. Maybe we can get one of the boys to grab you a glass of water? I know how the heat can sneak up on a body this time of year..."

The drill salesman scowled. "I'll be fine. Just didn't dress for the weather, is all. Besides, my good man..." John Henry was almost impressed by just how many square inches of vitriol the man was able to pack into those last three words.

John Henry unhooked his legendary hammer from its designated spot on his belt loop. He couldn't help showing off just a little. John Henry spun his hammer around in his fingers the way Jax Meteor twirled his electric six-shooter.

The crowd went wild.

The salesman rolled his eyes.

Mr. Everett raised a small silver triangle. He cleared his throat.

"Gentlemen? Are we ready?" Mr. Everett asked.

"Ready as I'll ever be," John Henry answered.

Mr. Everett nodded. "That's the thing about this little beauty... it doesn't matter how I feel. I could be tired, sick—Hell, I could be asleep—and the miraculous Pneumatic Steam Drill would still get the job done in no time flat."

"I'll go ahead and take that as a 'yes'," Mr. Everett said. He rang the triangle.

And our man John Henry too off like a bolt of greased lightning. He swung his hammer like the fate of the world depended on him (because, honestly, it kinda did), hammering steel spike after steel spike into the Earth with but a single strike of his mighty mallet. John Henry's muscles bulged so much; they threatened to pop through his flesh. He breathed so heavily in between swings, an old woman in the crowd fainted because there wasn't enough oxygen to go around.

On the other side of the aisle, the salesman fought back a yawn. All he had to do was press a button on the big, brass bastard and then walk alongside the thing as it did all of the work. Every time the machine punched a railroad spike into the ground, it did it at the exact right interval, in only a single action, using the absolute optimal amount of pressure.

But our man had a surefire way of making sure he wasn't intimidated by the infernal robot's—admittedly impressive—work pace. John Henry conducted his behavior in the contest the way he conducted his behavior in his everyday life: he didn't pay one lick of attention to what anyone else was doing. He kept his head down, and focused on doing the best possible job he could on his own work.

But even ol' John Henry had his limits. When the steam drill salesman pulled a pack of Morley's out of his breast pocket, and lit a cigarette using one of the sparks that was generated by the steam drill's strikes, several members of the crowd audibly gasped. And that caused ol' John to look up, and see for the first time what he was up against.

Saying that the steam drill was a thing of pure, efficient power might give one the wrong idea of what it looked like when it was in action. Sure, the machine ran like literal clockwork—but its execution of its task wasn't a smooth, non-violent process. The ridiculously high-tech motor that kept the device in motion generated so much power, the machine shook like it could blow apart at any second. The harder it worked, the more it appeared to snort steam through the vents located on either side of its undercarriage. Its steam-based innards made such a high-pitched, high-pressure sound as they worked their black magic, the resultant sound resembled something close to the warning cry of a furious zoo animal.

Taking all this in for the very first time caused John Henry's knees to buckle. Sure, he had taken on literal monsters before—but at least those hairy abominations were flesh-and-blood. This motherless machine was something else entirely. John Henry must've read at least two hundred trashy Science Fiction magazines in his life, and not even those could prepare him for the existential horror that overwhelmed his rational mind as he went to war against an honest-to-God unfeeling robot adversary.

John Henry started to falter. At first he fell one spike behind his Satanic, steam-powered opponent. Then two spikes. Then, somehow between blinks, it was ten.

"Don't beat yourself up about it, John," the salesman quipped in between drags on his cigarette, "you're just a man, after all..."

The way the salesman said it, like there was something wrong, something inferior about being a man. And that filled John's heart with an existential dread that soon alchemized into a white-hot, burning rage.

For the first three quarters of John Henry's life, he would've given anything to have his basic, innate humanity acknowledged. Now, after all of those years, it had been...and John would be damned if he was going to let any machine, or monster, or anything else take that away from him.

"Foreman?" John Henry yelled over the sounds of clanging steel and venting steam.

"Yes, John Henry?" Mr. Everett shouted back. "You doin' okay, son?"

"I'm doing just fine, sir," John Henry replied. "So fine in fact, I could use another hammer."

The crowd gasped.

Luckily, several of John Henry's co-workers had brought their work-hammers to the race, to wave in the air as a sign of solidarity. One of the men handed their hammer to Mr. Everett, and Mr. Everett used both hands to toss the hammer to John—who caught it in one.

With one hammer in each hand, ol' John Henry got to work with a quickness that'd make a hurricane blush. He struck one spike after another—barely pausing to take a breath in between. The iron heads of his hammer glowed bright orange, and his muscles bulged so huge his shirt chose burst rather than embarrass itself by attempting to contain him.

"Move, damn you!" the salesman shouted, as he kicked the steam engine with his boot, giving the shiny, new leather its very first scuff. "Move!"

And move the machine did—but not as quickly as John Henry. As John neared the finish line, he took once last glance at the throng of well-wishers cheering him—and Humanity, as a whole—on, and pushed himself even harder. So hard, in fact, that his heart exploded like a blood-filled, veiny hand grenade.

But not before he hammered his final railroad spike into the ground. Seconds before the steam drill was able to do the same.

John Henry won his race, but lost his life.

And that, of course, that is a downright, certified tragedy. Nobody in their right mind could argue otherwise.

But John didn't die in vain. Mr. Everett kept his word, and managed to keep his crew manned by human beings, rather than machines, for another two years (until he was fired and replaced heartless hombre named Kit Chesterfield, who was as infatuated with the almighty dollar as the vampires John Henry tussled with were obsessed with blood).

John Henry gave up the ghost, yes. But he died with his boots on. He went out like a man. And, most importantly, he left an epic story behind.

✝✝✝

Gentle reader, you and I live in a world in a world of skeptics, naysayers, and atheists. There are more than a couple so-called "experts" (more like "professional party poopers", if you ask me) in our day and age who claim that a man named "John Henry" never actually worked the rails. Or even drew breath. They saw that all of the various larger-than-life legends attributed to our man are actually an amalgamation of the achievements of five, ten, maybe even twenty wholly different people.

And that's because we no longer live in an era of heroes and magic. Instead, it's fashionable to disprove our legends with science. And to use scandals to discredit our heroes.

I'll tell you what—if ol' John Henry lived in our times, he wouldn't have to wait around for a steam drill to break his heart.

But, lucky for him—and for us—John had the good fortune of kicking the bucket back when folks were still capable of believing in something greater than themselves. Word of John Henry's incredible trials made the rounds, spreading from town to town the way the vampire virus only wishes it had. No matter what color or creed you were, John Henry's name became synonymous with heroism. In a new world, starved for a mythology to call its own, our John Henry joined the ranks of Paul Bunyan, Johnny Appleseed, and Bigfoot in the new American pantheon of tall tales. So much so, that you're reading about him right now, more than one hundred and fifty years since he last put hammer to railroad spike, in a collection of pulp tales not unlike the "Jax Meteor" paperbacks John used to enjoy.

And if you thought John Henry's life was wild, you'll never believe what happened to him after his death.

But that, my friend, is a story for another time...

THE END

THE MACHINE AGE

Ever since I was a (precocious, unbearable) little kid, I have been obsessed with mythology, folklore, and ghost stories. My gateway into this type of fare was the Stan Lee and Jack Kirby THOR comic, which teamed up the Norse God of thunder with the various costumed crusaders of the mighty Marvel mythos. I initially assumed that Thor (and, by extensions: Loki, Sif, Odin, Heimdall—all those colorful characters) were inventions by those two aforementioned Jewish gentlemen from New York.

When my school librarian informed me that Thor was, in fact, a thousands-of-years-old religious figure, it shattered the borders I had set up in my mind in regard to what was real and what was make-believe. Why was Thor real, but not Captain America? What did that mean about Santa Claus, Saint Michael, Bigfoot, Robin Hood, and The Tooth Fairy?

My confusion only grew when I started comparing the various myth-sets of the world, and found that they had more in common than not. Things like world-cleansing floods, subterranean punishment-dimensions, and tyrannical giants were echoed across cultures that had no way of communicating with—let alone plagiarizing—one another.

To young me, this was more than enough proof that magic exists.

Present-day Eric is a little more sophisticated than that. Having read the works of Carl Jung, Joseph Campbell, and Jordan Pedersen, I (very begrudgingly) acknowledge that the similarity in the myth-sets of the various tribes of humanity could be explained by the fact that we've all working with the same neurochemistry.

But there's still a little piece of me, in the very back of my adult brain, that is sure that if every culture from England to China has stories about dragons, then surely the shadows of this world contain more secrets than our modern minds would care to admit.

In the story you just read, JOHN HENRY VERSUS THE VAMPIRES, two men (one Chinese American, and one Mexican American) swap stories about their culture's respective vampire mythologies after meeting the even-weirder-than-fiction monster who inspired them all.

Regarding John Henry: is there any greater figure in American Mythology? I don't think so. In fact, as the years tick on, John Henry's theme of "Man vs. Machine" only becomes more relevant, while Paul Bunyan (deforester), Johnny Appleseed (distributor of non-indigenous wildlife) become more "problematic."

I think about John Henry whenever I see that another cashier at my neighborhood grocery store has been replaced by an annoying self-checkout terminal, or whenever one of those R2D2-like delivery drones rolls past me on the sidewalk.

Someday The Machines will overtake us, and inherit the earth. And maybe they'll invent their own mythologies, and tell their own stories. But, until then, John Henry exists to remind us to hang on to our Humanity as long as we're able.

✝✝✝

Eric Esquivel - lives in Los Angeles, California with his tiny white cat and tiny white girlfriend.

He is a graduate of The National Hispanic Media Coalition's screenwriting and theatre programs.

Eric has written extensively for Animation, Comics, Young Adult Literature, The Theatre and Video Games. Previous clients include Actionopolis, Archie Comics, Avid.ly, Boom Studios, DC Comics, Dynamite, Endemol Shine Boomdog, Fox News Latino, Frederator Books, Heavy Metal Magazine, IDW, Nickelodeon Magazine, Papercutz, Red Games, Scholastic, Somos Arte, Spookshow Records, Starburns Industries, Vertigo, Zenescope, Zoomob, etc.

Twitter: @ericMesquivel
Instagram: @eMeComics

THE LORD'S WORK

BY HARDING McFADDEN AND IRIS HAWKINS

The rain *pit-pit-pitted* on his tin pot hat to the tune in the shoeless man's song.

> "Some*times* a *light* sur*prises*
> The *Christian while* he *sings;*
> It *is* the *Lord* who *rises*
> With *Healing in* His *Wings.*"

The soles of his earth-browned feet were tough and leathery, taking no notice of the roots and rocks and cast aside thorns that he walked over as he moved across the thin country lane. His clothes were old and patched; hand-me-down's many times over before they'd been handed to him. The water skin across one shoulder was half full, and the sack across the other held food, rope, his hatchet, his bible, flint and steel, and the seeds. His face was merry, alight with a love greater than that available to man on this fallen world. He wasn't bothered by the weather, nor by the gray clouds and darkening sky that lived hand in hand with it, but rather seemed to revel in it. This was the day the Lord had given, after all, and who was he to cast shadows at it?

He'd been traveling the highways and byways for so long, spreading the Word and planting his orchards that he couldn't quite reckon what state he was in just then, but it didn't much matter. All the world was your destination when how you got there was the worthy part. Though stopping and looking around, pulling an apple from his sack and taking a hearty bite, he simply couldn't reckon the place. He'd been here before, he was sure, but when or where it was? Not a notion.

Shaking his head in acceptance of a lost memory, he took another large bite, and continued on his way, humming and singing all the while. A particularly large raindrop exploded on the silver handle-tip of his tin pot hat, sending fragments of glistening water into his half-opened eyes, causing him to chuckle at the irony of it. Grinning widely, he singsonged,

> "When *comforts are* de*clining,*
> He *grants* the *soul* again
> A *season* of clear *shining,*
> To *cheer* it *after* rain."

He ended with a grateful look toward the heavens, and a hearty, "Amen."

Lightning cracked the sky, splitting it like a torn celestial seam, afterword sending the land into comparative blackness, blinding the shoeless man, if only for a moment. Never breaking his easy stride, he asked aloud, "Is there something bothering you this day, Lord? Some task you've set ol' Johnny?"

To his left and right, all along the country road, but thinning as it crested the nearest hill, ran the trees, as thick a cluster of growth as he'd seen anywhere in the wilderness. White oak and red maple mixed with cedar and birch until the horizon was a hidden mystery. Were not he walking on a cleared path, he'd have felt like the first man to trek these lands, white or red, though the feelings of isolation were not to last.

In a whisper on the winds, his father's voice spoke to him. "My son," the voice said from out of the trees to his left, from the darkness that lived there. "Come to me, my son."

Shaken, he reached into his bag, and laid a comforting hand on the worn black covers of his Holy Bible, and called out, "Would that my father was here, but he's with the Lord, his mortal remains buried most of a continent away from here. So no father nor angel be you. That being the case, get behind me Satan."

At the center of the lane he stood, back straight, though not prideful. He was filled with peace, but not by his own making. Looking into the darkness of the trees, seeing in his mind's eye every imaginable demon lurking there, he prayed, "'Fear not, for I am with you; be not dismayed, for I am your God; I will strengthen you, I will help you, I will uphold you with my righteous right hand.' Father, in all things let Your will be done, and if it be this darkness that You have set before me, then for Your name's sake, I will meet it with all valor. In Your name I pray, Amen."

For another long moment, he stood there looking into the darkness, and though he still felt alien eyes upon him, he felt that he could wait no longer. Over the crest of the hill, he felt certain, lay his next destination, so to it he must go, to whatever fait awaited, on his endless quest to do the Lord's work.

†┼†

The smoke came into view before the cabin, and for the first time, Johnny was aware of not only the chill in the air, but also the near total absence of wildlife sounds. In the very far distance, he could just make out the rumblings of deer and warren-seeking bears, but closer to him, there was not so much as the chirp of a bird, nor the rustle of ground cover or leaves that told of squirrels or chipmunks or snakes. The autumn was setting in, but was still far enough off that nothing would be hibernating as yet, or explain why the birds had left the area. The land here was afraid, down to its marrow, and nothing was in evidence that could be elsewhere.

The cabin was simple. Situated in the center of the small clearing, it was made of the trees felled to make room for the settlers. Not large by any stretch, it would undoubtedly be cozy within, and in the depths of the onrushing winter would test the mettle of whoever stayed there. The four walls were chinked tight, the door appearing solid and sturdy, but it was the small window that gave him pause. Situated to the left of the gray stone chimney, between it and the door, the window was boarded up, letting in no light. This was no makeshift shutter, to keep out the elements, but a barricade, against something else. What? He wondered, then reminded himself of the voice in the woods.

Coming midway through the clearing, he stood out in the open, making himself seen, before yelling out, "Hello in there!" No matter how unnerving the circumstance, he simply couldn't help but sound cheery and hopeful. It was in his nature, and always had been. No matter the situations he'd found himself, no matter the monsters of the earth that he'd found himself nose to nose with, he'd always found himself high of spirits, elevated like a man Saved.

Inside the cabin, he could just make out the sounds of uncomfortable scrabbling, and words spoken in haste partially hidden beneath the unstopping pitter patter of the rain. While those inside decided whether to answer him or kill him, Johnny looked up into the still darkening sky and breathed a deep breath. Many were the ways he'd rather spend a day than walking in the rain, but looking up into that roiling vortex of a black and gray sky, with its tentacular strobes of lightning, feeling the overwhelming awe that came to him when he remembered just how small he was, and how unimaginably vast God was, he was grateful for the respite. Lest pride seep into the heart, it was always good for a man to be humbled by nature.

In time, a simple lock was removed from inside the cabin, and the door was opened a crack. The eye that looked out was starkly blue, and tired. Aged beyond its years, by situation and circumstance.

"Who are you?" called a weary voice from inside. In its exhaustion was also threat, and also undoubtedly a loaded musket.

"Those as know me call me Johnny," he called back, keeping his ground. He'd neither advance nor retreat, lest he give this frightened man an excuse to shoot him down. Though his soul was prepared to die, he'd rather not go at the cause of a frightened misunderstanding.

"What do you want?"

"In truth, I think to talk. I've been many days' traveling, without any voice but my own for company, and I'd revel in better company." He smirked at his self deprecating joke, though no chuckle came from within the cabin. "Y'see, I've been walking this country of ours, meeting those that would meet me, planting my orchards, and spreading the Word. And every so often I come across something that needs a special touch. Like that voice that talked to me in the woods not too far aways."

On instinct, the man at the door started to close it, but was staid by another voice from inside. A woman's, sounding every bit as tired and terrified as the man. In a rush, she begged, "Algernon, please, you can't leave him out there for that foul thing. To let it get him wouldn't be Christian. At least let him stay the night."

Looking into the sky again, Johnny took notice of the spreading darkness. Not only the storm, but the sun conspired against him, the day being much further advanced than he'd realized. In no time at all, an hour at best, the sun would have settled down behind the hidden horizon, leaving him to the machinations of nature, and the hungry things that harbored there.

With an audible sigh, the man opened the door wider, calling out, "That's a strange hat."

Chuckling, Johnny replied, "It's a strange day."

Words heavy, the man asked, "Are you a dangerous man?"

With a smile, Johnny answered, "Yes, sir, I am."

Confused, but sensing no antagonism coming from their unexpected guest, the man moved back from the door, and beckoned Johnny inside.

With a nod of thanks, the shoeless man moved toward the cabin, thankful for the warmth promised within, and promising God to do what he could to help its inhabitants, for His glory.

The inside of the cabin was simplicity itself. A basic fireplace, small but more than large enough to warm the single room. Four beds, bunked two to a side at the end opposite the fireplace. An antler rack mounted to the wall near the beds upon which hung coats, and in the topmost antlers the musket that Johnny had known would be here. A small table, only just large enough to eat on. And on the earth floor a bear skin rug that felt wonderful on his bare feet.

The inhabitants of the cabin were a mix of confusions. A man and a woman, they were dressed in what would have been fine clothes, if far from the finest, back east. Both in their middle thirties, he a handsome man if worn down by months of distress, she a lovely woman in an earthy way, both with brown-blonde hair, but obviously not related. A husband and wife, they were each others' whole world, but they shared a sense of emptiness, as if something real and whole had been stolen from them. Johnny looked the cabin over, and his eyes fell on the two extra beds.

"We don't have much food to offer, I'm afraid," the woman said, ever the hostess, even out in this unforgiving wilderness. She held herself well, but was obviously very wearied.

"No need to worry about me, miss," Johnny told her, unburdening himself of his bags, and removing what food he had. Apples, and corn cakes, and salted meats littered the small table, not much by any standard, but enough for a banquet for these intimate confines. Their eyes widened looking at the food, but both had too many manners to just reach out and take things. Sensing their reluctance, Johnny offered, "Take whatever you want. The Lord provides, and it's my honor to share." He picked up an apple, and took a bite, letting them know that what was his was theirs.

With smiles of gratitude, and hardly repressed tears of joy, they dug in, filling themselves, but not glutinously. Algernon and his wife had been so long with nearly nothing, that even this simple fare was heavenly, and more than once they thanked him. Each time, he gently reprimanded, "I only give what's been gifted, praise the Lord."

When each was full, and there was hardly anything left on the table, the three sat back, the men on the bear skin rug, the woman on the end of a bed, and breathed in a sigh of contentment. For the moment, each could convince themselves that things were normal for them, that they weren't in the middle of nowhere, surrounded by shadows that lived and talked and hungered.

Reluctant to break the respite, Johnny asked, "What has happened here? And where are the two that slept in those bunks?"

When his wife began to cry, Algernon said, "Please forgive my Anna. We've been far too long living under this horror, and it wears the nerves something horrible."

"Nothing to forgive, I beg you," Johnny told them. "Though please unburden yourselves. Even the stoutest can break under too heavy a weight. I have an ear, so: let me hear."

With a nod, Algernon stood, and fed more wood into their dwindling fire. The rain outside had grown steadily in the time that they'd eaten, and with it came wind that battered the cabin, though its timers were sturdy, and it would take more than the storm had to give to reach them inside.

"We set out from Philadelphia," Algernon explained. "Nearly a year ago. The city had just gotten too unwelcoming, unfriendly to any civilized person."

Johnny nodded. He'd been to Philadelphia, as well as Pittsburg, and Boston, and many a city, and had never felt at home in any, regarding them as places where humility goes to die. Was it any wonder, then, why he made so much of his life in the wilderness?

"There were four of us when we set out," Anna said, calming herself with great effort. She'd be no weak sister of circumstance, not while any steel still lived in her spine. "Algernon and I; my brother, Ambrose, and his wife Martha."

"We sold everything we had," Algernon continued. "Our homes and businesses and most of our clothes."

"Anything we could do without," Anna said. "We kept some clothes, some books, our family Bible."

"Sold it all, and purchased the supplies we'd need to make a fresh start of it on the frontier," Algernon said. "Bought a pair of horsed, a wagon, more supplies than could be used in a year, and set off on a beautiful Monday morning in May." With this last, his eyes closed, remembering the day vividly, like it was right there in front of him, more real than anything he'd seen since.

When Algernon was silent for a bit too long, lost in thought more than was good for any man, Johnny brought him back: "All the supplies that you could need, and…?"

Lowering his head, eyes open now but seeing nothing, Algernon continued, "For months we traveled. More than once we were forced to trade in the horses for new ones, we were so fearful that they wouldn't make the rest of the trip. But then, one day, we were here. I cannot tell you why we decided to stop and build here, but when we set foot upon this ground, we felt at home, like this was the place that our steps had brought us. We started building the cabin that very day."

"Algernon and Ambrose took the saws and axes and started cutting down trees to make the clearing, and in no more than two days had built these four walls," Anna said proudly. There was love in her eyes when she looked at her husband, and though he returned the gaze in turn, there was a sadness there, as if he couldn't help but se sure that she'd have been better off had she never met him. "The roof came soon after, until by the end of that first week, we were all cozy and fine inside. It was like the first steps in our next journey."

"Things started to turn sour shortly," Algernon said. "This land is full of holes, some small and some deep places. I fell in one of the small ones, and broke my leg. For nearly a month I was laid up with pain and fever, and I feared that I would never make it. Many days are lost to me, and I dreamed the most horrible things. That left it up to Ambrose to do the hunting for us."

Nodding sadly, Anna said, "He went out one morning, to bring back whatever meat he could find, and never returned. That's been months."

"And Martha?" Johnny pressed. "His wife?"

"Mad with grief," Anna whispered.

"For the longest while," Algernon said, "she'd pace the house, mumbling to herself. At first, it was prayers that he was alright, and that he'd find his way back to us. But, in time..." He broke off, awkwardly, causing his wife to continue.

"In time," she said, "she began to say horrible things about us. About me. She'd say things about how unfair it was that I still had a husband, while her's was lost to the wilds. She became bitter, and hateful. For a short while this stopped, when she tried to..." Now it was her time to be awkward.

Johnny filled the silence: "She tried to take your husband for her own? Or tried to convince you to share him?"

Her face red with embarrassment, Anna said, "Share, at first. When we said that it would be sinful, she tried to take him all for her own, like he was Ambrose. When we told her that she needed to stop, she flew into a rage, began shouting about *needing a man of her own!* Said that she'd do anything to have someone all her's, that no one could take away. She became violent, throwing things at us, ruining out precious flour, pouring the milk that we'd traded a homesteader a day's travel away into the fire. We tried to restrain her, but before we could, she'd run out the door, and into the wilds, shouting that she'd find her Ambrose, that he was all hers, and no wilderness could take him from her."

Sadly, Johnny nodded along with the story. He'd seen it before, city folk driven to madness by the struggles and hardships of the frontier, losing their minds to the endless isolation. Many was the person who just wasn't cut out for it, and there was no shame in that. Only pity, at having tried and failed and lost it all, in the end even losing yourself.

"How long after that did the voices start?" he asked them.

In surprise, Algernon asked, "How do you know about the voices?"

Throwing a thumb over his shoulder, in the direction of the country road, he told them about the voice of his father. Though it was more than that. "I've traveled a lot, doing what I do, and in a lot of places, there's myths and legends that'd make your blood run cold. In a little town in Ohio, there's a story about a man who took up with a woman against her will when the state was first being settled. In the end they'd killed each other, and over their bones grew a haunted tree that brought woe to all that visited it. In Tarrytown there's a story about a headless Hessian who rides the highways seeking his head, and taking many a one from a lonely traveler until his is found. Yes, there's many a tall tale. But in my travels among the red men, time and again I've heard a story about a beast that'd been a man at one time. Driven by greed and avarice, he'd gluttonously see to his own wants in spite of the needs of the tribe. In his greed,

...SHE TRIED TO TAKE HIM ALL FOR HER OWN.

he finds himself in the deepest woods, starving and alone, stumbling upon a poor stranger, who he kills and eats whole. But in so doing, he's damned himself to an eternal life of hunger, growing thinner and thinner until he's nothing more than tight skin stretched over bones, unable to ever ear enough to stop his starvation. The Cree people call it a wendigo."

✝✝✝

From out of the storming night came suddenly the voice. From the distance of the tree line, it whispered, "Anna, my sister, come to me."

With a stifled shriek, Anna jumped to her feet, and backed against the wall furthest from the door. Her hands were clenched into white-knuckled fists, and pressed against her mouth. For his part, Algernon had gained his feet and taken the musket down from its place upon the antlers. Keeping the muzzle aimed toward the ceiling, he nevertheless kept his eyes locked on the sturdy door. Still on the bear skin rug, Johnny sat upright, and removed his bible from his bag.Turning without looking to Matthew 6, he recited,

"Our Father which art in heaven, Hallowed be thy name.
Thy kingdom come, Thy will be done in earth, as it is in heaven.
Give us this day our daily bread.
And forgive us our debts, as we forgive our debtors.
And lead us not into temptation, but deliver us from evil: For thine is
the kingdom, and the power, and the glory, for ever. Amen."

Turning his eyes upon the frightened woman, he said, "That is not your brother. Even if it had once been, it is no longer. By some unknown tragedy, your brother was lost, as well as his wife. This harsh land took them, and in their place let loose the demon speaking to us from out there. But, have no fear of it, for the Lord is with us. And if He is standing with us, then nothing in all of hell might stand against us. You must believe that."

Calming, Anna nodded, forcing her hands from her mouth. She sat again on the edge of the bunk, placed her hands in her lap, closed her eyes, and whispered the twenty-third Psalm:

"The Lord is my shepherd; I shall not want.
He maketh me to lie down in green pastures: he leadeth me beside the
still waters.
He restoreth my soul: he leadeth me in the paths of righteousness for

his name's sake.

Yea, though I walk through the valley of the shadow of death, I will fear no evil: for thou art with me; thy rod and thy staff they comfort me.

Thou preparest a table before me in the presence of mine enemies: thou anointest my head with oil; my cup runneth over.

Surely goodness and mercy shall follow me all the days of my life: and I will dwell in the house of the Lord for ever."

"Anna, my sister," came the knowing response from outside, closer now than before. "Why do you not answer me? Do you no longer love me?"

Her voice elevated by fright, she said her prayer again: "The *Lord* is my shepherd..."

Over and over again she said the words, enriching her strength, and angering the entity outside. In frustration, it raged at the storm. In between shrieks and wails, it spoke to the three of them, its voice changing as it shuffled through person after person, trying to dig in its talons of despair and disbelief. Upon hearing the voice of Martha shouting at him from the storm, saying many cruel and perverse things, Algernon left his spot in the center of the room, and knelt in front of his wife. Musket on the floor between them, he took his wife's much smaller hands in his, and prayed with her.

"My son," came the voice of Johnny's father then. "My son, why do you reject me? Love your father, and obey him. Open this door for me."

Standing, one outstretched hand upon the coarse wood of the door, the other holding open his bible, Johnny read, speaking of the acts of the apostles, quoting the many letters of Paul, reciting from memory the words of his Lord and savior. Tirelessly, he went on, Hour after relentless hour, regardless of what sounds assaulted him from outside. So engrossed was he in his recitation, that he took no notice when his mother's voice bellowed disturbing vitriol at him through the door.

In response, in fury and frustration, the beast outside threw itself against the walls of the home, banging and pounding until its body must have been a bloody tatter. But injuries seemed not to bother it, as it went on like that throughout the night. The sturdy walls of the home held, as did the slanted roof upon which it ran for a frightening while. The door held fast, the simple wooden barricades supporting it.

When, after nearly a full night had passed, the assault on the building finally stopped, the silence was nearly as jarring as the cacophony had been. But even under the thundering of their own heartbeats and whispered prayers, just on the other side of the door, inched from Johnny's fingertips, they could hear the heavy, ragged breathing of this unseen beast.

"I'll have you," it whispered then, deep and guttural. "I'll feed you pain as if from a bowl full of thorns."

Then, quite suddenly, it left, ran off, the sounds of its emaciated feet moving away at great speed, into the deep woods with the coming of the first rays of the sun.

†††

Exhaustion overtaking them, the three found some comfort in sleep, Algernon and Anna beside each other on the bear skin rug, Johnny leaning against the wall beside the still burning fire. Though the husband a wife slept dreamlessly, Johnny's dreams were dark and troubled. In them, he stood in the center of an endless, dark wood, the shadows moving around him, protected only by a beam of heavenly light that reached down from the sky to envelope him. His eyes on the unreadable pages of his opened bible, he could hear those things that sniffed out his blood moving ever closer. In spite of himself, he could feel the cone of light shrinking inward, the muddled pages growing ever more dim, as his strength and faith deserted him bit by bit, like a peeling onion, until at last the light was only just covering him. Refusing to believe that this was to be his fate, he gripped the book tightly, looked into the darkness, and shouted, but all for nothing, as his cries of defiance fell on deaf ears. Inch by inch the darkness moved in, and the horrors that lived in it, until at last the light flickered out, and he was left alone, just him, and them, and an eternity of pain.

With a sigh, he woke, cracking open his eyes. Surveying the room, he saw that Algernon and Anna were still asleep. The fire was dwindling, the incoming cold being what had pulled him from sleep. Smirking, he sat up, rekindling the fire, and thanked the Lord for the chill. Looking at the door of the house, he whispered, "To enter my dreams, you must be quite desperate, demon. But it will do you no good. You cannot dwindle my faith. For I *know* the Lord is with me."

The fire raging once again, he saw to what food they had left, and had set the table by the time his new friends had roused from their much needed slumber. Sitting up awkwardly, with shy words of thanks, they sat at the table, said prayers over the food, and ate. There wasn't much, and even with careful rationing, they'd be left with nothing by the next day.

"I'll be leaving your company today," Johnny told them, leaning away from the table when still far from full so that his hosts might eat better.

Frightened, Anna asked, "But what of the... the...?"

"I'LL BE LEAVING YOUR COMPANY TODAY."

"The wendigo," Johnny finished for her. "It won't be about in the light of day. John tells us, 'For every one that doeth evil hateth the light, neither cometh to the light, lest his deeds should be reproved.' No, I'll take my leave soon. Though I'll not leave you in a lurch. I plan to go further into these woods, to find the beast."

Now husband and wife were shocked, bolting to their feet and looking down at the sitting man as if he were mad. Calmly he sat there, listening to their complaints and worries.

"You can't," Algernon scolded. "Even if you're right, and it won't bother you in the light of day, it'll be dark in no time at all, and you'll be its victim. To go out there is foolish, akin to suicide."

"Yes," Anna pleaded. "You can't go. You'll die, horribly. And alone."

Johnny smirked at them. "I'm never alone. And if I'm to die, if this day is to see my end, then I would rather it be on my feet, nose to nose with this enemy, for the glory of my Lord, rather than hiding until starvation takes me. I'll be doing this, with or without your blessing. That being the case, I'd beg two favors from you fine people. Pray for me, that my task might be complete before I am spent. And if I'm not suited to it, then leave this place when the sun rises, lest you find yourselves lost here forever. It'll be hard traveling, no matter which way you go, but there's a settlement, small but Godly, not twenty miles from here, to the south. If you don't see me, please go. I'll meet my maker with a smile, if I know that you've at least got a chance to live."

In short order, and with no action wasted, Johnny had packed out his few belongings, and was at the threshold of the cabin, saying his goodbye's to his kind hosts. Very briefly they'd known each other, yet in that time they'd had an experience that would stay with them all. He would remember their love for each other in the most difficult of circumstances, and they would remember his faithful certainty and optimism. A fair meeting, indeed.

Still the sky drizzled, there being no reason for surcease of chill and misery.

The men walking together a few feet from the house, while Anna looked on from the safety of the door, Johnny turned to Algernon, and said, "How long have you had the musket?"

Hefting the gun, Algernon answered, "Most of my life. My father fought with it during the Revolution. When he took down his shingle, he gave it to me."

"And you're proficient with it? You can hit what you aim at?"

"I like to think so. Though there's a part of me that thinks it should go with you, into this danger that you've set yourself."

Johnny shook his head. "No, where I go, I have all that I'll need. You keep that with you, should I be unsuccessful." He looked past his new friend, at the lovely, faithful woman that watched them. "Remember this, though: Should the worst happen, it is your responsibility to die for her, if only to give her a few more seconds to reach safety. No matter how ghastly your fate, it is preferable to her death. To let her die first, or to sacrifice her so that you might live, is a failure. It not only makes you less of a man, but hardly better than an animal. Do you understand?"

Algernon nodded. Far from being offended by the other man's worlds, he was uplifted by them. He was not sure if any of them would survive this, or if they would fall to the same fate as Ambrose and his wife Martha. If this was to be their end, however, this stranger had given him words to help him die well.

Unable to help himself, Algernon embraced his new friend, hugging him like a lost brother, gone for far too long. When at last they separated, he stood there, in the center of the clearing, watching as Johnny strode boldly into those dark, haunted, infinite woods, toward whatever fate none could know.

†††

The woods had a breath and exhalation all their own, the ever-present wind creaking and groaning the ancient bark, breaking the weakest twigs, and bowing thinner branches. The roots ran deep, but the feeling was that even they quivered in their earthen home. A chill passed through Johnny as he walked, half from the elements, half from known devils. He ignored it, and moved further and further into the autumn mirk.

Feeling that he was being watched by a thousand eyes, he said, "I reckon you're there. You've always been there. If not as this wendigo, then as another kind of monster, back to the very dawn of man. Kin to the serpent. Since we fell in the Garden, you've been there, you and your kind, to nip at our heels, and tempt us toward sin. That's right, isn't it?"

The wind rattled the branches overhead, and that seemed to him affirmation enough. He stepped over an exposed root tall enough to have been a natural gate. On the other side of it, he nearly toppled into a hole where he'd expected good earth to be. Catching himself, and leaping the few feet across the cavity created by the raised root, he smirked, again chastising himself for his forgetfulness. Just the day before, Algernon had told him of falling in a hole nearby and breaking his leg. He'd said that the land was filled with such holes. Having almost experienced one himself, Johnny told himself to be mindful.

Dry leaves rattling past his bare feet, he took in a deep, bracing breath, and continued: "Many's the preacher that I've heard that blames all of the woes of this world on you and your dark master. Though it's not quite the case, is it?

Yes, you're the planted seed of our own destruction, but we're the fertile field, aren't we? Were we not so ready to forget salvation in favor of the pleasures of this world, you'd have nowhere to plant, would you? No, demon, you're not so much the invader that we'd like to imagine you. You're more the hired plow man, coming into our land by invitation. We've brought you on ourselves."

For a long while he lapsed into silence, as he was wont to do when thinking of the failures of his fellow man. The cruelty, and drunkenness, and debauchery. As a follower of Christ, he believed in the salvation, that it was available to all; he knew that a heavenly home was his final destination, as it could be for every man and woman. But as a realist he also understood that there were those who, even when faced with their impending mortality, even after living through the endless blessings of God's glory, would nevertheless settle back on their haunches, and allow themselves to be rushed away toward oblivion on a wave of sin and destruction. It was at times like these that a sort of melancholy overtook him, though never for long. Pulling himself out of his current funk, he sang:

"In holy contemplation
We sweetly then pursue
The theme of God's salvation,
And find it ever new;
Set free from present sorrow,
We cheerfully can say,
E'en let the unknown to-morrow
Bring with it what it may!

"It can bring with it nothing,
But He will bear us through;
Who gives the lilies clothing,
Will clothe His people too;
Beneath the spreading heavens
No creature but is fed;
And He who feeds the ravens
Will give His children bread."

"You believe in your god, my son?" his father's voice asked abruptly from the dark of the woods. From all around him came the words, as though he were not so much surrounded by the beast, but rather rested in its mouth, waiting for those terrible jaws to snap shut.

"I do, demon," Johnny answered, hand inside his bag, palm resting on his bible, fingertips on his hatchet. "As do you, so do not try to make me doubt. Even for a servant of lies, it would be simply too disingenuous of you."

"A loving god, my little Johnny?" Came his sainted mother's voice.

"Again: I do, demon, and no matter the voice you use, you'll not trick me into thinking you anything other than what you are. Neither my mother, nor my father. Neither one of Algernon or Anna's kin, though I suspect that you may well be one of them. Or at least *were*."

"I must know," voice drifted like molasses between the voices of his mother and father, Ambrose and Martha. "How might you believe in a loving god, who sees to your best, when He leaves you all alone in this wilderness... *with me?*"

Johnny smirked, looking all around casually, into the darkest shadows without fear. "You misunderstand, demon. He's not left me alone with you. Your master's left you alone with *us.*"

For many hours, his unseen traveling companion did not speak. In time, as the middle of the day approached, Johnny was left with the firm impression that he was indeed alone. Perhaps the demon had grown tired in its once-human shell. Perhaps the light of day, heavily filtered though it was as it reached down through the trees, was painful to it, and it needed to flee. He'd seen such when dealing with blood-suckers in the Virginia. Whatever the case, when he came at last to the first of the deep pits, he was quite alone, and he wondered if this was a boon, or somehow unfortunate.

The pits, like the one that he'd nearly fallen into, or the one that had broken Algernon's leg, were round, and in many cases dropped straight down into the earth, like they'd been dug there. Most were holes only a foot or so wide and delved perhaps three feet deep. Others, however, were many feet across, and dropped down twenty or more feet. A few, even standing right on the edge of, he couldn't see the bottom of, like they were tunnels leading to the very center of the world.

Some few of the holes seemed cut into the earth at angles, allowing Johnny to explore with little fear of becoming stuck. Still, out of caution more than fear, he'd tie the length of rope in his bag to a nearby tree, the other end around his waist, before looking too far.

In many holes he found animal bones, some incredibly old, some so fresh that they still looked wet. The fresher ones had chips in them, dug by ravenous teeth determined to get every last bit of meat from them. In a few cases, the bones were cracked open, the marrow sucked out. Though the skulls were the worst, their tops being bashed open, and the matter inside eaten along with the rest of the carcass.

In his travels, in particular in the northwest, he'd come across creatures that the locals had called 'Worm-Men,' short, stick-thin things whose long legs were all out of proportion to the rest of them. More than once he'd seen them, but never known them to be violent, or even to eat. Their time seemed to be passed in the digging of holes both large and small, identical to those he examined now. The Worm-Men may well have dug these holes, but they had nothing to do with the bones resting therein.

Passing early afternoon he found the remains of a human. Too scattered to gauge the size of, he nevertheless looked at the stripped bones and knew who he'd found. Like the animals, these bones had been stripped clean, the marrow sucked out, the skull crushed and hollowed. In some of the ribs, he could see signs of breaks that had nothing to do with the devourer, as well as in one of the leg bones, and along the right brow of the skull, apart from the removed bone, he could see a deep cleft, the wound that had done more to end the life of this poor soul than any of the others.

In sadness, he knelt beside the bones, gathering them into as close an approximation of their former station as he was able, and said a prayer over them. Gone on to reward or punishment long since, he couldn't let the finding of these remains pass without a remembrance of some sort, small though it might be.

Standing and wiping the dirt and debris of the tunnel from his hands, Johnny looked at all that was left of these mortal remains, and whispered, "Stay you in your rest, and forget about the woes of this world. The demon can't hurt you now, neither can man. The Lord bless and keep you."

When he left the tunnel, he was surprised to see how late in the day it was becoming. Looking around, mindful of the holes that hid themselves from him even then, his mind began to turn. A plan let itself be known to him, one that would take great luck, and much planning, but one that was possible, even with his limited means.

Eyes closed, he smiled, and turned his face toward the sky. "Your will be done," he said, and set about his work.

The woods were nearly black with shadow before the sun had fully set in the west. In a hollow provided by a massive toppled tree, Johnny had gathered many twigs and what dry wood he could find, and got a small fire going. The last his food was gone, but nature provided. There were some late season berries to be had, and mushrooms aplenty. The wind still pushed the world around, and even in his hollow the rain came at him, but not so much as to quench his fire.

The darkness breathed…

His back to the fallen tree, the dark of the woods all around, and the fire close enough to warm, he sat cross-legged, looking out into the endless night. Just past the light cast by the fire, he could just discern a shape moving in the darkness. Never did he try to convince himself that it was a trick of his imagination, because that way lie death. So, then, his visitor was coming for him.

"You see me, my son?" his father's voice asked from the shadows. "Simply wonderful." The shape moved, black against black, except where the firelight lit its approaching eyes, filling them with hellfire.

"I think that I know which of them you claimed," he told the shape, nibbling the corner of a mushroom. "I'd my suspicions when I talked to Algernon and Anna at the cabin. When they'd spoken of her brother, Ambrose, hunting in these woods, never to return. The loss drove his wife mad, they said. So mad that she took to the woods, herself, in search of her lost husband. And she found him, didn't she demon?"

"Indeed," came the voice of a woman, neither his mother nor Anna, that he reckoned to be that of poor, mad Martha.

"Starved, was she?" Johnny asked. "Half dead from hunger when she stumbled across his body in that hole? She'd missed him so much, needed him so much, and when she'd found him, it'd been too late. Was that the way of it?"

Silence for a handful of heartbeats, then: "Yes. So, so hungry. And all that meat, just waiting there. A bit riper than she was used to, but there."

"How long did she wait before you overcame her? How long until she took the first bite?"

"No more than a day," a masculine voice—Ambrose?—answered, with something like relish in its voice.

The glowing eyes seemed to float seven feet in the air, perhaps even eight. It had recently eaten, then. Forever starving, this beast could eat its weight and never be sated. As it feasted, it grew, so that it would always starve, no matter that it eat the world.

"Why bother the people in the cabin?" he asked it, though he knew the answer. He needed to keep it talking. Needed to anger it, until its last vestiges of reason had left it. "Anna was their kin. They'd have welcomed her back with open arms, no matter how she'd left them."

"Algernon," the feminine voice answered. "It wasn't fair that the woman have him all to herself. Not when he could be mine. Both of them could. All mine, to have, and love, and devour. To pull this hunger from me, in the name of their caring."

Across the fire, the shape moved closer, becoming more defined by the moment. Eight feet tall, yes, and stooped. Skin black and gray, pulled so tightly against thin bones that it looked like the flesh at elbows and knees would split in the bending. Its hips were narrow, its ribs outstanding, its breasts hollow and withered. Its nose was all but gone, the lips pulled back so far from the teeth that the dry gums could be easily made out, even at a distance. But the eyes, those fire-reflecting eyes, sitting deep in their black sockets were terrifying. In them all likeness to a human was lost, forever invaded by a creature from the deepest, most depraved pit in the underworld.

Nude but sexless, it stood across from him now, hardly six feet away, and towering. It looked so thin, even in its height, to hardly weigh as much as a bird, but when its feet touched the ground, they sunk in deeper than Johnny's would have. The weight of sin held it to the earth, where it rooted heavy, but he had no doubt that once in motion, it would be a lightning-quick sight to behold.

"Walk with me, my son," it said, looking at him from within those deep and endless sockets. It reached out a welcoming hand, and Johnny struck.

Slamming down a hand, he upset a thick stick that he'd had lodged beneath the fire, just enough earth built up between it and the flames that it was protected from burning. The fire and ash erupted from the blaze and landed squarely in the monster's horrible face. With shrieks of pain and fury, the wendigo launched itself backward, away from the pain and its intended victim.

All at once, before the ash had even settled, with the stink of burnt flesh all around him, Johnny was away and running through the black night. Behind him he could hear the horrible shrieks and growls of the beast, sounding somehow both human and animal. Amongst the noises filtered the words, "I'll have you! I'll have you in my belly!"

With great suddenness, the beast was after him. Though he dared not look behind, he could easily make out the sounds of its charging, bursting through dry growths, shattering thin trees, impaling itself on branches unnoticed. He could smell the burning and the sickly sweet scent of its blood, and hear the sounds of its breathing, heavy and heavier as it rushed him. As he came at last to the trap, he could actually feel its breath on his neck, and the stinging points of its outstretched fingers just touching the flesh of his back through his sweat-drenched shirt.

Headlong he leapt to the top of the unearthed roots, throwing himself into the void beyond it. It was so dark that he was effectively blind, and had to trust to the faithfulness of God like he'd never had to before. Beneath him, the pit dropped sharply, forty feet deep, fifteen across. Hanging over the exact center of the hole, knotted soundly in a thick outstretched branch, was his coil of rope, his lifeline, the single thing that would save him from a most horrible fate.

Hands outstretched, fingers splayed wide, he groped for the hanging rope, hoping that it would be where it should be, that it hadn't moved in the breeze or fallen into the hole, his knot being unworthy. When, miracle of miracles, his fingers made contact with the harsh fibers of it, he held on for dear life, feeling his hands burn as they fought for purchase before gaining it. His forward momentum pushed him further on, his legs flinging outward, his body launching into the deeper darkness beyond the hole.

When he hit the ground on the other side, and was brought up cold in a tangle of thin growths and brambles, he forced himself to turn, and listen. As he'd found himself airborne, he could hear the beast behind him, taken completely unawares, hitting the unearthed roots and tumbling with loud shouts and unholy oaths into the hole, where it struck bottom with a sickening crunch. For moments it stayed there, screaming at the night, before he could hear the scrabbling sounds of it beginning to ascend the pit.

Following the sounds, Johnny drew the hatchet from his bag, and perched on the pit's edge. In pain and agony, but unable to stop its pursuit of prey, the wendigo made its slow way up. For many minutes it climbed, digging broken fingers into the rough earth, until at last, Johnny could just make out a thin, skeletal hand reaching up out of the hole, not two feet in front of him.

The hand grabbing for purchase in the wet earth, too busy trying to escape to even notice Johnny. It was shocked when the sharp blade of the hatchet fell, striking off the fingers of the hand and a good bit of the meat behind them, dislodging the beast from its precarious perch. Again it fell, with a shriek born of pain and frustration, only to hit the bottom of the pit with enough force that even from his higher vantage point, Johnny could hear bones splinter and break.

He could hear it writhing where it had landed, too hurt to move now, crying pitifully. He knew that it wouldn't last. Creatures like this, he'd learned, were able to heal themselves from some of the most horrific injuries. The twitching fingers beside him on the ground would regrow even as these withered to nothing. The broken bones would set themselves. Evil would always beget more evil, either here, with this beast, or in some other form, but in the end they all amounted to the same thing.

Exhausted, Johnny allowed himself to drop to sitting, his body wet with sweat and rain, his breaths coming in great ragged gulps. More often than should have been possible, he'd found himself in situations where he'd had to run for his life. It never grew into a welcome sensation, but did have the added benefit of making him appreciate life, for all its ups and downs. After all, where there was life there was hope.

"Why?" Rose his father's voice from the pit. "Why do you so forsake me, my son?"

"Again, demon," he answered. "You are not my father. My father is in heaven, and in all too short a time I will see him again."

His mother's voice then: "But why do you fight? What is in this fallen world that it worth fighting for? Why not let them die? Why put yourself between the unsaved and peril?"

"Because that it our work. We are to go out and make disciples, who will themselves make more. We move ever outward, like a wave of light. We are to get between the unsaved and the Pit, and share the Good News. We are to be the shield that saves; the witnesses of the eternal salvation. If I had not put myself between you and them, I'd have lost my very soul."

"You'll lose that at any rate," a new voice, angry, feminine. "Before the worms have your shell, we'll have your soul."

"Impossible. My soul has been bought and paid for by the precious blood of Christ. It's not yours to have."

The long night passed, and all through it Johnny sat by the pit's side, wet and shivering, but unwilling to leave his watch. Hatchet always in hand, he hunched there, waiting for something to reach out from the darkness, but as the hours passed, and no such form drifted up out of the shadows, he began to wonder if the creature had been more hurt than even he'd hoped.

As the rain continued its endless *pit-pit-pitt*ing on his tin pot hat, he sang:

"Though vine nor fig tree neither
Their wonted fruit shall bear,
Though all the field should wither,
Nor flocks nor herds be there:
Yet God the same abiding,
His praise shall tune my voice;
For, while in Him confiding,
I cannot but rejoice."

Long about dawn, he first made out the faint sounds, beneath the rustles of nature, yet not a part of them. Like the gnawing of smoked meats married to the papyrus grind of ancient, dry teeth, it drifted up horribly, and the man of God shuddered. He knew what this was. He'd come across it before, and more than anything, it was his most detested part of one of these enterprises.

Seemingly a lifetime ago, he'd told Algernon and Anna, "In my travels among the red men, time and again I've heard a story about a beast that'd been a man at one time. Driven by greed and avarice, he'd gluttonously see to his own wants in spite of the needs of the tribe. In his greed, he finds himself in the deepest woods, starving and alone, stumbling upon a poor stranger, who he kills and eats whole. But in so doing, he's damned himself to an eternal life of hunger, growing thinner and thinner until he's nothing more than tight skin stretched over bones, unable to ever eat enough to stop his starvation. The Cree people call it a wendigo."

What he hadn't told them was that he'd encountered them before, coming not only from the Cree, but from all cultures. He'd seen the foul beasts dispatched by those that knew how, and had removed some few himself. And in better than half of his experiences, he'd had the discomfort of knowing on what they feasted when there was no other food available.

"What have you started with?" he asked it, voice thin. Always was the hope that if he could only keep it talking that it would stop its horror, and expire of the gnawing hunger that engulfed it.

"The feet," his mother's voice replied sweetly. "Then onto the legs, my dear. They're ruined from that last fall, and will be no good to me at any rate."

"They won't fill you," he reminded it. "Not even if you ate the lot."

Voice garbled, its mouth full of meat, it asked, "How is it that you know so much about what's happened to us?"

Us. Not What's happened to me. No. Us. Many. Legion.

"I've shouldered the responsibility of dispatching many a demon before you."

"Though never a woman?"

He shuddered, uncomfortable that this nether creature could still see into his fallen, but saved, soul. "No," he admitted. "Never a woman. Many a man, and more than a few animals that'd gotten the devil in them. But never a woman. Have you infested many women?"

A juicy chuckle slithered up to meet him. "Many," it told him, its voice sickening and suggestive. "Many times many. Nothing much is sweeter. Nothing much."

Closing his eyes, Johnny began, "Our Father, who art in heaven…"

Over the sounds of the creatures munching and crunching, he prayed for hours. His voice grew horse in the day's chill, and he was certain that a cold was overtaking him. He'd be wracked with fever before too long, and perhaps not up to the task that still awaited him.

Feeling sluggish, he stood, and moved his way around the pit, to the base of the tree from which his rope still hung. Climbing it, and shimmying his way out into the thick branches, he unknotted his rope, and coiled it around his weak arm. Sitting there for a long moment, he looked down into the darkness of the pit, and was certain that he could make out darker shadows moving within the gloom. Though they did not move well. Perhaps it was nearly time. Perhaps there wasn't much left to eat.

Descending the tree, he knotted his rope lower, and left the remaining coil

"WHAT HAVE YOU STARTED WITH?"

at the cusp of the pit. Gathering wood, he started a fire nearby, building it larger and larger until a nearly dangerous blaze warmed the cold day. It felt good to him, and took some of the stiffness from his bones.

With great care, he brought more wood, larger chunks that should burn well and long, to the fire, and once they were well-lit, began dropping them into the pit. All the way down, they sputtered, but most stayed alight, illuminating the bottom, and giving him a good view of his responsibility.

Drawn into the center of the pit, shunning the cleansing fire that rained down from all sides, it was a true horror to behold. It was larger than a normal person, the body that remained having enlarged as it had eaten itself, guaranteeing that it would never be anything less than starving. In the time that it had been down there, it had devoured its legs completely, all of its lower body to the bottom of its ribs, and one of its arms. All that remained was the other arm, a fraction of the trunk, and that horrible head.

"I'm coming for you, demon," he told it. "Are you ready to return to your master?"

For another great while, he dropped more and more burning wood down on it, shrinking its world until it could hardly move an inch. It was trapped, well and truly without hope, and its executioner had just dropped a rope into its final resting place, to climb down and kill it.

Nearing the end of his strength, Johnny climbed down his rope, dropping into one of the few places that he hadn't built up the fiery wood. Gazing over the flames, he saw the orange-sized eyes looking out at him. Stout of heart, he was nevertheless taken aback by that stare. Here was a hate not possible in man. This was something deeper, and older, and purely Fallen. Armageddon given flesh.

Hatchet in hand, with a great leap he was over the fire, his skin a glistening sheen, sweat pouring from him. He landed solidly, and in an instant was attacked by his foe.

Reaching out its single arm, the creature took firm hold of his shirt and pulled him toward it. Cavernous mouth open and seeking, it gnashed its teeth at him as he kicked at it, and struck with his hatchet. Parts of its face came away in ragged sheets as he hacked at it over and over, but it seemed not to feel the injuries. Like an unstoppable object, it pulled him in closer and closer. It was than, when it felt most confident, that he struck.

While his hatchet had its uses, it would be hard pressed to destroy this beast so intent on devouring him. He could hack and slash for hours, and it would keep coming. He'd known this, even before dropping into the pit. What he'd needed to do was get close, so that a little bit of nothing could do its job.

Hardly a foot away from its seeking jaws, Johnny suddenly threw his head forward, ramming the silver tip of his tin pot hat's handle full into the center of the wendigo's forehead. With a sizzling hiss, the silver struck home, and dug in so deeply so quickly, it may as well have been a hot knife, going through the butter of the horror's head. In agony, it let go of its intended prey, and reached for the offending pot.

Seizing his opportunity, Johnny struck again with the hatchet, hacking the remaining arm free at the elbow, before bringing it down again and again with all the force he could muster on the monster's withered neck. In moments, the head came free, and the remains of the body dropped to the floor, twitching but not dangerous.

Setting to work on the remains, he sectioned the torso with his hatchet and rolled the bits into the fire where they burned like dry kindling. The last of it set burning, he turned his attention on the head, where it lie on its side, eyes wide, alive and watching him.

Careful to not get near its mouth, he pulled his tin pot hat from its forehead, and knelt before its hateful, terrified eyes. Breathing deeply, his body shaking, he said, "I'm not talking to you, now demon. I'd have words with the woman that you stole. Are you there, Martha?"

There was a flicker in the eyes as he spoke the name, but he could not be certain that it was the poor woman, or simply another trick of the demon. Not that it mattered, he supposed. If there was even a chance to get to her through it, he had to take it.

"I wish I'd have met you in better times, Martha," he told her. "I've met your kin. Algernon and Anna. Fine, God-fearing people. I'm sure you were much the same. Likewise your Ambrose." For a moment, something else washed across the desiccated face. Sadness? A moment, then gone.

"I can only pray that in your life you were saved," he continued. "I must choose to believe that you were, and that before you were corrupted by this evil that you were aware of the salvation that has been gifted you. I must choose to believe this. You understand, don't you?"

Suddenly, the head raged, screaming without noise, writhing as much as it could with no body to move it. Slowly, Johnny retrieved his tin pot hat from where he'd sat it, and poked the silver tip at the head. "Be silent, demon," he insisted. "I am not talking to you."

Holding the hat in his lap, he said, "I'm sorry that you had to end your days like this, Martha. I could wish that you'd have had a long, happy life with your kin, filled with love and the laughter of children, but we both know that wishing is useless, and that we must each shoulder the burdens that are laid upon us. This has been your final burden, and I relieve you of it. And I can only hope that you can forgive me for shouldering more now, as I do what must be done.

May the Host of heaven carry you now on your way."

Standing on shaking legs, he reached behind the gargantuan head, and took half of the papery flesh stretched there. Lifting it, he took it to the largest of the still-burning fires, and placed it into the blaze. It sparked instantly, and burned brightly and hotly, smoke erupting from it like the soul of Martha running to her reward.

When the remains had burned to nothing, he forced himself back up the rope. It took the last of the strength and will that he had in him, but he knew that if hadn't done it then, that he'd have died down in that hole. The fever had fully taken him by the time he'd rolled up onto the wet ground, and for many hours he lie there, shaking and coughing and incoherent.

Crawling, he made his way back to the great blaze that he'd started earlier, pulling what wood passed his way along with him. The fire had shrunk somewhat since he'd gone down into the pit, but was still lively enough to burn what he threw into it. Before the fever fully incapacitated him, he'd gotten it burning fully again, forcing some warmth into his frozen body.

✝✝✝

Nearing midnight, wracked with fever and feeling as ill as he'd even felt, Johnny was ready to give up the ghost. He'd later think it ironic that this was just what would save him.

He'd fought the good fight, had spread the Word, and was sure in his delirium that the Lord was coming to take him home. The insistent rain still fell, not in torrents, but in a steady mist that penetrated to the bone. The fire was long since gone, and what clothing he wore was more hinderance than protection. It was just then, as his eyes grew dim, and the stars overhead began to flicker and fade, that the light drifted into his vision from all around.

The darkness that had engulfed him for hours vanished in comforting waves, floating away like smoke in a breeze. In its place came the woman. Floating into his line of sight from everywhere at once, she smiled down at him with love and comfort. She was beautiful in her plainness, her clothes robes of purest light. Her hair was dark, and drifted around her head as if in water. Though it was her face that drew his eyes. There was kindness there, and thankfulness, and appreciation. He'd never seen her before, but looking up into her angelic visage, he knew her like they'd spent a lifetime in each others' company.

Unable to speak, he mouthed her name: "Martha."

Smiling broadly, she nodded, and drifted down to lie on the ground beside him. All at once, the chill left him, and his muscles settled from their shivering. His breathing became more steady, and the pains that had so filled him receded to near nothingness. Turning his head with dreamy effort, he looked into her friendly eyes and felt complete calm.

This must be death, he thought, untroubled.

She looked into his eyes, and though she spoke no words, told him, *No.*

†††

When he opened his eyes again, the storm had at last passed, as had his fever. He was drenched to the skin, and weak from hunger and his broken fever. Without sitting up, he reached into the bag that still encircled his shoulder, and took out a bruised but delicious apple. Taking a hearty bite, he smiled and thought, *Thank you Lord for this bountiful harvest.*

By stages he rolled onto his stomach, then up onto his knees, and after many failed, humorous efforts, to his feet. He was shaky, but with great effort, found that he could put one foot in front of the other, and make slow, but steady, progress back the way he'd come.

During the hours that remained to him before sundown, he trudged along, never less tired, but ever more steady on his feet. When he set his camp for the night, it was with great thanks. He set a small fire, ate some late-season berries, and slept the sleep of the just.

It was nearing noon the following day when he came at last to the cabin of Algernon and Anna, and he was hardly surprised to see smoke coming from the chimney. They'd stayed, rather than running as he'd suggested. Hardly seeming to be lazy people, he assumed that they'd had more faith in him than he'd had in himself.

As before, coming midway through the clearing, making sure he was seen, he called out, "Hello in there!" His voice sounded weak to his own ears, and more than a bit scratchy, but it carried nevertheless. In seconds, the door was opened.

Algernon and Anna erupted from their home and greeted him like the prodigal son. He embraced them both, and gratefully allowed himself to be shown into the cabin. Seated before the warm fire, he told them of what had happened since their parting, and both sat there and listened. There were tears upon learning the fate of Anna's brother Ambrose, and initially mixed feelings about Martha.

"You have no need to feel ill toward her," Johnny told them solemnly. "Whatever that demon in the woods might have been, it was not your Martha.

She died when she found her husband, and in her place walked something else. She was no less a victim than was Ambrose, and should be mourned just the same."

The couple nodded sadly, and sat next to each other on a bunk, holding hands, but unwilling to show more affection in front of someone else, regardless of circumstance. He had no doubt that when he left them, the following morning, they'd be each others' shoulder to cry on, for as long as it took.

With the dawn came the time for goodbyes, and he wasted no time. Hefting his bags, he left their home, moving back toward the woods and his future. They walked with him.

"Where are you off to?" Anna asked.

"Wherever the Lord leads me," he told her truthfully, smiling. "And you? You've had a bad start of it, and no one would blame you for turning back."

"No," Algernon said. "We've made it this far. I suppose we'll survive here."

"Yes?" Johnny asked.

"Yes," Anna answered. "After all, what fresh hell might find us worse than the one we've already been through?"

The shoeless man smiled at her, though there was melancholy in it. What fresh hell, indeed?

Reaching into his bag, he asked them, "Might I impose upon you to do me a favor? Should you find a nice spot in your clearing of this space, might you plant some of my seeds? I leave them most places I go, to give me something to come back to. Mayhap it'll give me an excuse to visit you some time."

Taking the small offered bag of apple seeds from their departing guest, Anna said, "I'd be delighted. If you promise to visit, any time you're near."

Tipping his tin pot hat by the handle, Johnny bowed slightly, and promised, "I shall. You may count of in."

Hefting his bags, he turned from them sprightly and walked into the woods, his earth-browned feet tough and leathery and better than most shoes. Neither root nor thorn bothered them. Likewise, the chill of the day gave him no pause. As he disappeared into the woods, his voice drifted up into the heavens, earthy and alive:

> "Some*times* a *light* sur*pris*es
> The *Christ*ian *while* he *sings;*
> It *is* the *Lord* who *ris*es
> With *Heal*ing *in* His *Wings.*"

Where he was going didn't even enter his mind. He would go where he was needed, and would do the work set out before him. Even in his solitude, he was not alone. He traveled with a song in his heart, and a love impossible to man.

"Lead me where you will, Lord," he said. "And I will follow."

The road of the Soul is unknowably long,
Though it's always a dead-end road.
It's a merciless thing, but still laid out with care,
Where the devil and God have both strode.
-"Epigraph" by Harry Hawkins
-for Naomi and Eleanor,
with love.

THE END

Afterword:

American mythology is every bit as interesting as world mythology, plus (for someone like me who hates to travel) has the decided benefit of being within driving distance. So when I saw that this new volume of Pulp Mythology needed one more story to complete its contents, I jumped at the opportunity to write an American mythological horror story.

I'm honestly not sure what pulled me toward Johnny Appleseed, as opposed to Paul Bunyan or Molly Pitcher or countless others for this first co-creation with my youngest, Iris, other than the memory of both of my girls having "Johnny Appleseed Grace" sung to them on long family road trips all through their youth. Those are fond memories for me, and if I were a betting man, I'd reckon that there's where the nugget was found.

As to the why of the wendigo, still wanting this to be a distinctly American mythological horror story, I wanted to use a distinctly American monster. There were many choices available—mothman, bigfoot, skin walker, etc.—but for some reason the wendigo just felt at home here. I'm very well aware that there are many related myths that don't exactly mesh up with what I've written here, but then again there's many related myths that don't mesh with each other. That being the case, I've tried to keep the critter recognizable, while not adhering to any of the many divergent descriptions of our big bad.

Twice now, my oldest daughter, Eleanor, and I have written stories that the fine folks at Airship 27 have seen fit to publish in their superior volumes. Those, for anyone who'd interested, are "The Ghoul Strikes!" in *Mystery Men (& Women)* volume 7, and "Devil's Donations" in *Mystery Men (& Women)* volume 10. While we were finishing up the second of these, Iris, asked when she and I could write something together. A great kid, I am loath to let her down, so when I started plotting "The Lord's Work," I asked her if she wanted to help out? Boy, did she, and with gusto!

For the better part of a week, she and I sat and talked through the basic plot, me telling her some of what I had in mind, she saying more helpful things, like, "Wouldn't it be cool if..." And she was right. Together, we fleshed out the narrative, but the majority of the end was all hers. I got to writing on October 19, and for the next week and a half (excluding Sundays) she came to me for day-by-day updates, making sure I was trucking along with our little fright tale. And in no time at all, thanks to her gentle nudges, it was all done.

In my co-writes with Eleanor, because of the kinds of stories we were telling, I had the opportunity to just let go with the violence, and let the blood run down the screen. In the case of "The Lord's Work," that kind of an approach just wouldn't fly. Besides the fact that Iris is only 9, and I'd like her to be able to read something that she helped write before she's a teenager, and given the nature of the hero, I thought a more subtle approach would be better. As such, for the vast majority of the story, we decided to keep the monster, and most of the horrors attributed to it, off camera. And even when violence was done in front of the audience, I tried to keep it as bloodless as possible.

And a final note, for any who might be interested: Throughout the story, our old pal, Johnny Appleseed, sings a song. That song, by William Cowper (1731-1800), is called "*Joy and Peace in Believing*", and was found quite by accident. In the first draft, Johnny was singing "*Johnny Appleseed Grace*," which I'd always assumed was an older hymn, but turned out to be something owned by Disney. Needless to say, I didn't want to use any copy-written lyrics, and trusted to Robot Overlord Google to help me out. I needed something with weather imagery (specifically rain for the opening scene), and stumbled across this perfect choice. I'd never heard of it before, but had heard of William Cowper, and decided almost instantly that this was the song to use. I hope that you found it a worthy choice, and the story worthy of the lyrics.

I guess that's all for right now, other than to thank you for reading our story. We both sincerely hope that you enjoyed it, and were able to spend a few scary moments with us without regret. Have a wonderful day.

-h & I

†††

HARDING McFADDEN & IRIS HAWKINGS are a father-daughter writing team from Pennsylvania. "The Lord's Work" is their first published collaboration, with many more on the way. They are currently outlining a time travel story filled with fascists and dinosaurs and family values that might very well be the best thing you ever read (who knows, right?). All other things being equal, they just hope that you enjoyed their story.

www.ingramcontent.com/pod-product-compliance
Lightning Source LLC
Chambersburg PA
CBHW070820250626

47170CB00006B/2170